All at once the telephone rang, and Zelda rose from the table to answer it. "Hello, Spellman residence."

She listened thoughtfully for a moment. "You say that Hilda Spellman just won an all-expenses paid vacation to Hawaii? The tickets are in the mail? Thank you, I'll let her know."

"Yay!" shouted Hilda.

Zelda hung up and turned to Sabrina. "Okay, what's going on?"

Sabrina shook her head puzzledly. "I don't know how this could backfire, but Dreama just cast a spell that made all superstitions worthless."

Both Hilda and Zelda gasped out loud and looked horrified. Hilda put her hand to her mouth and turned to Dreama. "You cast a bad luck spell on the entire mortal population!"

Sabrina, the Teenage Witch™ books

Available from ARCHWAY Paperbacks

Sabrina
The Teenage Witch®

Knock on Wood

John Vornholt

Based upon the characters in Archie Comics

And based upon the television series
Sabrina, The Teenage Witch
Created for television by Nell Scovell
Developed for television by Jonathan Schmock

AN ARCHWAY PAPERBACK
Published by POCKET BOOKS
New York   London   Toronto   Sydney   Singapore

AN ARCHWAY PAPERBACK *Original*

 An Archway Paperback published by
POCKET BOOKS, a division of Simon & Schuster, Inc.
1230 Avenue of the Americas, New York, NY 10020

ISBN: 0-671-04070-7

First Archway Paperback printing September 2000

10 9 8 7 6 5 4 3 2 1

To Nancy

Chapter 1

Lights glared down on the sparkling green football field, giving it a golden glow under a dark autumn sky. The crisp air carried the gooey scents of hot apple cider, popcorn balls, and cotton candy. Fans in the bleachers talked loudly, competing with the noise on the field. The marching band blared the Westbridge High fight song, as the football players charged onto the field for a kickoff.

On the sidelines, a guy in a vegetable suit danced in front of the crowd, trying to keep in step with the peppy cheerleaders. What an embarrassing mascot, thought Sabrina; but they were the Fighting Scallions, after all. They were supposed to be the Fighting Stallions, but there was a misprint on the jerseys.

High up in the bleachers, Sabrina and Dreama crawled over people, trying to find seats. They were late as usual. Sabrina had been working at the coffee shop, and Dreama had just been late, her head in the clouds. But they had finally met at Sabrina's house and zapped themselves to the school in time to catch the fourth quarter.

There's a big crowd tonight, thought Sabrina as she plunked herself down on the hard bleachers. Harvey couldn't see them from the field, so he wouldn't know how late they had been. Now he wanted her to come to all the games, because he had been playing a lot more since scoring a touchdown a few weeks ago.

"Wow!" said Dreama, shouting over the music and noise. "I didn't see all these people when I was here before. Where did they come from?"

"The team won last week!" answered Sabrina happily. "It was the first game the football team has won in years, and now everyone wants to see if they can do it again."

"Was it really that long since they won?" asked Dreama.

"They hadn't won a single game since I've been here," answered Sabrina, "and I'm a senior. What's the score of this game?"

"We just scored another touchdown, and we're ahead!" crowed a student in front of her. "Can you believe it?"

"A miracle!" exclaimed Sabrina. "And Harvey's in such a good mood after they win, although he's too sore to do anything but sit."

After the kickoff, the teams huddled for the first play. The Westbridge players were dressed in green and white uniforms, and they were on defense against the dreaded Warren Hootowls, dressed in black and gray.

"You know," said Dreama, "I think I'm beginning to understand how football is played. It's a very friendly game, really."

"Friendly?" asked Sabrina doubtfully. "Are we talking about *American* football?"

"Yes, it's so sweet!" exclaimed Dreama, clasping her hands together. "First the boys get into two groups and hug each other. Then they go line up across from the other boys . . . like they're going to ask them to dance. Then they all rush forward and hug each other again. Only they're so rough about it that they knock each other down. Then some of them pat each other on their bottoms."

"That's about it," said Sabrina. Dreama was a witch who had been sent to Sabrina to learn how to do magic and live in the Mortal Realm. Sabrina figured that someday she might be able to teach Dreama to do magic correctly—maybe—but she doubted if Dreama would ever understand mortals.

"Didn't you notice that funny-shaped thing

they play with?" asked Sabrina. "It's called a football."

The other witch frowned. "I thought they were playing hot potato. They throw it around to each other, and nobody seems to want it. And when they kick it, they kick it as far away as they can. The only thing I don't understand is why we have to sit on these hard benches."

"It's a macho sport," answered Sabrina. "Even the fans have to be tough."

Suddenly, the crowd started cheering, and everyone leaped to their feet and waved frantically. "It's an interception!" blared the announcer over the loudspeaker. "Brad Alcerro has the ball and is racing for the end zone!"

The crowd screamed and punched each other as Brad scored another touchdown for the Fighting Scallions. Sabrina hated to admit it, but Brad was a good football player. He was also her nemesis, because he was a natural-born witch hunter. Even though he didn't know what he was looking for, he had come close to discovering her secret several times.

"Look! They're all hugging Brad!" exclaimed Dreama. "What a great game!"

Westbridge had just gone ahead by fourteen points, and people were celebrating as if they had won the Super Bowl. It seemed incredible, but they were about to win *two* games in a row! They weren't the worst football team in the country anymore. Even the mascot in the scallion suit didn't look as geeky as before.

Half an hour later, the game was over, but the party went on for a long time. Sabrina and Dreama went down to the school to wait for the players outside the locker room. Before this, only girlfriends, parents, and ambulance drivers ever waited for the players, but tonight there were little kids, sports fans, even newspaper reporters.

When Harvey, Brad, and the rest of the players came out, a great cheer went up. A bunch of kids surrounded Brad, asking for his autograph. When some cute girls rushed up to Harvey, Sabrina instantly cut in. She had broken up with Harvey for a while, and she wasn't going to lose him again.

"He's taken! He's taken!" she shouted, pushing the girls away. Sabrina grabbed her boyfriend and gave him a big, sloppy kiss.

Normally she liked kissing Harvey, but tonight his chin was all rough from not having shaved, and he . . . well, he smelled bad.

"Uh, Harvey," she whispered. "I think you forgot to take a shower."

"I didn't forget," he answered cheerfully. "I'm not going to take a shower—none of us are."

"Why?"

Harvey looked very serious for a moment. "You know that athletes are sometimes a little superstitious."

"No kidding," grumbled Sabrina. "Just because you eat anchovies before every game."

"Right!" said Harvey, thinking she understood. "The players decided that none of us will change our socks or underwear, or take a bath, until we lose a game. We've won two games in a row, so it's working!"

"It's working, if you want to gross people out. And I thought you were smelling a little ripe last week." Sabrina crossed her arms and looked over at Brad, who was showing a girl his muddy T-shirt. "Let me guess whose idea this was: Brad's."

"How did you know?" asked Harvey in amazement. "Brad always has great ideas for team spirit. Like he suggested that we all go out for pizza at the Slicery. You girls can come, too."

Maybe greasy pepperoni would drown out the boys' reeking smell, but Sabrina doubted it. "Okay, just give me time to catch a cold."

"Oh, you're always so funny, Sabrina." He gave her a good-natured cuff on the chin. "A bunch of us are going in Brad's car—you want to come?"

"No," she answered quickly. "I mean, I came with Dreama, so I'd better go with her."

"See you there." Harvey joined his football buddies just as Dreama walked up to Sabrina.

Dreama sniffed the air. "I think the Porta-Potties overflowed again."

"No, that awful smell is my boyfriend and all the other football players. They've decided not to take baths or change their underwear or socks until they lose a game."

Dreama looked shocked. "I didn't think mortal boys changed their socks."

"On rare occasions, they do," muttered Sabrina. "But the football players won't even do the bare minimum—take a bath. This whole thing is just a silly superstition."

"What's a superstition?" asked Dreama.

Sabrina sighed. "How am I going to explain this without making mortals look stupid? Okay, sometimes they *are* stupid. You know that mortals don't have any magic, but they still believe strongly in good luck and bad luck. They think they can bring themelves good luck by doing—or not doing—something. Like if they find a four-leaf clover, that's good luck. But if they break a mirror, that's bad luck."

"That's not so stupid," said Dreama. "It's a really bad idea to break a magical mirror. I know, I've done it."

"They don't have magical mirrors," answered Sabrina. "They don't have anything magical—they just *think* they do."

Dreama frowned. "Then they're poor, deluded fools."

"But they're still cute." Sabrina took the arm of her fellow witch and steered her toward the sidewalk. "Let's get some nose plugs, then go eat pizza."

When Sabrina and Dreama arrived at the Slicery, they found half the football team sitting out on the curb. They were eating pizza out of boxes, and a Closed sign was visible in the Slicery's window. Strangely, most of the seats in the restaurant were filled with diners.

"Hi, Sabrina...Dreama!" called Harvey, jumping to his feet.

Sabrina had a paper bag in her hand, and she quickly shoved it behind her back. "Why are you eating out here?"

"They wouldn't let us stay inside," he whispered. "Take-out only."

Brad jumped to his feet and angrily kicked a pizza box. "I say we take our business elsewhere. We'll show this lousy place when we're city champions! Then they'll be begging for us to come back, and we'll eat at some other pizza joint."

"It may be harder in a month or two," said Sabrina.

Brad approached her, his dark eyes flashing. "Are you saying that you agree with them—that we smell bad?"

"No, not at all," said Sabrina. Without thinking, she brought up her hand containing the paper bag, and Brad noticed it.

"What's in the bag?" he asked suspiciously.

"Uh, just a few cans of deodorant. You didn't say anything about not using deodorant, did you? It's Right Guard!"

Brad flapped his arms and looked at Harvey with exasperation. "She's your girlfriend—can't you talk some sense into her? Get her with the program." Brad stomped off, grabbing a slice of pizza from one of his teammates.

Harvey looked disappointed as he gazed at Sabrina. "You know, it's not just a superstitious thing. It's a solidarity thing, a way for the team to be special and stick together."

"Another few days of no bathing, and you'll stick to everything," said Dreama helpfully.

"Come on, guys, let's go!" shouted Brad, motioning to his teammates. They marched off into the parking lot, taking their pizza boxes with them. Harvey started to go with them, then he looked back at Sabrina, obviously torn about what to do.

"Go on with the team," she told him. "Enjoy your victory. I'll see you tomorrow."

"You're the greatest, Sabrina!" He smiled sheepishly and dashed after his smelly buddies.

After they left, Sabrina heard rustling in the bushes, and she turned to see two more girls from school, Barbara and Jill. She wondered why they were hiding, when she remembered that they also had boyfriends on the football team.

"You can come out now," said Sabrina. "They're gone, but their scent lingers on."

Jill stepped out of the bushes, holding a small atomizer. "I wanted to squirt some perfume on Billy, but I think the deodorant is a better idea."

"They wouldn't go for it," said Sabrina. "They take real pride in smelling bad."

"It can't be legal for them not to take showers or change their underwear," complained Barbara. "There's got to be a law against it. Or maybe a school rule."

Sabrina snapped her fingers. "Right! A school rule. All we have to do is go see Mr. Kraft and tell him about it. He'll make them take showers. Didn't he used to teach hygiene?"

Jill frowned. "I hate to turn them into the principal, but do we have any choice?"

"No, you don't," answered Dreama "The drugstore was sold out of nose plugs."

Sabrina clapped her hands together. "Okay, we'll meet at Mr. Kraft's office in the morning. Tell all the other girls—bring as many of them as you can."

"Sure thing, Sabrina," said Barbara. "Thanks."

"I feel better already," added Jill, squirting perfume in the air.

When the two girls had left, Dreama turned to

Sabrina and whispered, "We could always use witchcraft on them."

Sabrina shook her head. "No, I don't want to try witchcraft on Brad—he might sense something. Besides, I think Mr. Kraft will make them clean up their act."

On the restaurant door, the Closed sign suddenly flipped to Open, and Sabrina asked, "Want to get some pizza?"

"Sure!" answered Dreama. "That's one mortal custom I understand."

Chapter 2

☆

Mr. Kraft listened patiently to the nine teenage girls gathered around his desk. He nodded with sympathy as Sabrina described how awful the boys smelled, and how they were going for *another* week without bathing. Maybe it would even be longer, if they kept winning. Mr. Kraft wrinkled his nose with obvious distaste.

"So isn't there some kind of school rule against this?" asked Sabrina. "I mean, there's a rule against everything else!" The other girls nodded in agreement and looked pleadingly at Mr. Kraft.

The principal smiled like a walrus who has just eaten a bucketful of fish. "Let me get this straight. This silly superstition keeps the girls away from the boys, and makes the boys think they can win every football game. Tell me again why I'm supposed to be against it?"

"Because they reek," answered Sabrina. "They're grossing everyone out."

"No problem." Mr. Kraft opened a drawer on his desk and took out a large gas mask. "Sorry, I only have one of these. Now go away."

"Are you sure there isn't a rule that all students have to be washed and bathed?" asked Dreama.

Kraft laughed so hard that he had to wipe tears from his eyes. "Ha! Ha! A rule that all students have to be washed and bathed! What dimension are you from? Oh, that's a good one, Miss . . . Whatever-your-name-is."

The principal snapped his fingers and jumped to his feet. "But you have given me an idea. If our team really believes they can win every game, then maybe they *can.* We play Sunnyside High in a few days, and I'm going to call up the principal and offer her a little wager. I bet we can keep winning. Knock on wood!" He rapped his knuckles on his wooden desk.

Sabrina rolled her eyes. "Don't tell me you're superstitious, too."

"Maybe I won't have to take a bath either," said Kraft with a satisfied grin. "Now get to your classes, all of you!"

Morose, the girls filed out of the principal's office and scattered in different directions.

"At least they're still brushing their teeth," said Jill.

"For now," grumbled Barbara.

Sabrina and Dreama hung for a moment in the hallway, and Dreama shook her head in amazement. "I can't believe how superstitious they are. They have no magic, but they think silly things like knocking on wood are going to help them?"

"I would love to teach them a lesson," whispered Sabrina. "Show them how geeky they are with their superstitions. You can't get magic by finding a horseshoe! Although around Christmastime, there's a really cool superstition about mistletoe—"

"There must be something we can do," said Dreama worriedly.

"We could hit the army surplus store and see if they have any more gas masks." Sabrina sighed and shook her head. "Walk home with me after school, and we'll figure out what to do."

"Okay."

"Gotta go!"

Sabrina rushed off, leaving Dreama to ponder the problem. She didn't hear the novice witch say to herself, "You're right, we really should teach those boys a lesson."

* * *

As if the day wasn't going badly enough, it rained on Sabrina and Dreama as they walked home from school. Sabrina thought about using magic to get them home faster, but she could see that the rain wasn't going to last long. By the time they reached her house, it had turned into a light drizzle, and the sun was peeping through the clouds.

They found Salem, Sabrina's black cat, sitting on the front porch. The front door was open, but he was staring intently at the sky. Unlike most pets, Salem was a witch's familiar, and he could talk. He had once been a warlock himself, but he had been turned into a cat for trying to take over the world too many times.

"What are you doing?" Sabrina asked her pet.

Salem cocked his head and answered, "I saw a rainbow a few seconds ago, and I want to see if it comes back."

Dreama smiled and said, "Yes, rainbows are really pretty."

Salem snorted derisively. "I don't care if they're pretty—I just want the pot of gold at the end of the rainbow. I could *use* a pot of gold."

"Not you, too!" groaned Sabrina. "That's just a silly legend . . . a superstition. There is no pot of gold at the end of the rainbow."

"How do you know?" asked Salem suspiciously. "Have you ever been at the end of a rainbow?"

Sabrina pointed her finger, and a burst of magic twinkled at her fingertip. Suddenly a huge, dazzling rainbow shot across the sky, and the tip of it plunged into the dirt in the Spellmans' front yard.

"See. No pot of gold," said the witch triumphantly.

"Spoilsport," muttered Salem. The cat curled his tail with disdain and strolled into the house.

Sabrina sighed and motioned to Dreama to follow her in. When they reached the living room, they found a ladder standing in the center of the room. One of her aunts must have been trying to change a lightbulb in the overhead fixture. They could use magic, but they liked doing household chores to keep from getting too lazy.

"It's supposed to be bad luck to walk under a ladder, but watch me." Ducking, Sabrina walked right under the ladder, and nothing happened. "There! Another ridiculous superstition debunked. I should have a TV show."

They walked into the kitchen to find Aunt Hilda making a salad and Aunt Zelda adjusting the oven. Salem sat on the counter, swishing his tail excitedly, and Sabrina knew that dinner must be coming soon.

"Hello, girls," said Aunt Zelda. "How was your day?"

"Oh, I've had better ones," muttered Sabrina.

"It was interesting," answered Dreama.

"How about your football team!" exclaimed Aunt Hilda. "Did they kick some tail last night, or what?"

"Yeah, it was a great game," said Dreama. "Lots of hugging."

The timer went off on the stove, and Zelda reached for some potholders. "The chicken's done." She opened the oven and took out a roasted chicken simmering in its own juices.

"Be still, my heart," breathed Salem, inching closer to the steaming bird.

"Back off!" cautioned Hilda, giving the cat a stern glare. "The chicken is for us. You get chicken by-products, also known as cat food."

"But that's nothing but the beak and the feathers," complained Salem. "And their little scrawny claws."

Brandishing a big knife, Aunt Zelda hovered over the chicken. "Okay, I might as well carve this lovely bird."

"Don't break the wishbone," said Aunt Hilda. "You always break the wishbone, and I like to pull it for good luck."

"Aunt Hilda!" scolded Sabrina. "Don't tell me *you* believe in silly superstitions?"

Her aunt looked chided. "Well, of course not. It's just fun to pull the wishbone . . . and you never know."

"Sabrina's right," said Zelda. "There's nothing

to mortal superstitions except for a lot of folklore and repeated behavior."

"If that's so," countered Hilda, "then why do you always wear your lucky suit when you appear before the Witches' Council?"

"Repeated behavior," explained Zelda. "I wore it once, and things went well, so I keep wearing it. The famous psychologist, B. F. Skinner, did a lot of experiments, and he found out that even animals are superstitious. He knew that pigeons would perform certain tricks if they were rewarded with food, and he wondered what they would do if he gave them food every fifteen seconds—for doing nothing.

"The pigeons were soon running around in circles, hopping on one leg, flapping their wings—all thinking this behavior was making the food come. In reality, it came if they did nothing at all, but they couldn't believe that. The experiments even worked with people. He set students in front of a keyboard, and if they pressed the 3 key, they got a nickel. If they waited a few seconds and pressed 3 again, they got another nickel."

Zelda laughed. "But the students didn't realize it was that easy. Most of them developed elaborate key combinations, such as 4–3–2–1–2–3–4 or 3–3–2–2–1–1–2–2–3–3. They took great pains to memorize the pattern and repeat it each time, when all they had to do was press one key."

"That's exactly the trouble I'm having," said

Sabrina. She explained to them about the boys refusing to bathe or change their underwear while they were on a winning streak. "It's the *team* that's winning the games, not their dirty socks!"

"That's a classic case," said Aunt Zelda. "I don't know what you can do, unless they start losing again."

"I don't want to make them lose," answered Sabrina glumly. "But football players need to take a shower every now and then."

Dreama snapped her fingers. "Why don't we make it rain real hard, then zap them out of their uniforms for a while?"

Sabrina shook her head. "I don't think West-bridge High is ready for nude football."

"Okay," said Dreama, undeterred, "why don't we steal their underwear while they're sleeping and wash it for them?"

Sabrina wrinkled her nose. "I'd rather not do a giant panty raid. Besides, this whole idea was Brad's, so I can't say anything against it. And I don't want to risk using magic on Brad."

"No, don't do that," cautioned Hilda. "Don't use any magic around that witch hunter."

Salem growled. "Will you people stop talking and carve the chicken? Or a black cat is going to cross your path."

"I'm not really hungry," muttered Sabrina. "I'll eat later, if you don't mind. I'm going up to my room. Want to come, Dreama?"

"Sure," answered the novice witch.

"Good!" said Salem. "More for me!"

The girls climbed up the stairs and passed the door to the linen closet. "Want to go to the Other Realm?" asked Dreama. "Maybe that will cheer you up."

"No thanks," answered Sabrina. "What would cheer me up is a boyfriend who doesn't smell like a locker room."

"This whole thing is ridiculous. I'm going to teach those silly boys a lesson." Dreama tugged on her earlobe and said a rhyme: "No superstition will ever work; anyone who thinks so is a jerk."

Sabrina blinked at the younger witch. "Did you just cast a spell?"

"I sure did," answered Dreama proudly. "I just made all superstitions worthless."

"But they were already worthless."

"Oh." Dreama frowned in thought for a moment, then shrugged. "Then I guess I didn't do anything at all."

Sabrina stomped her foot on the floor. "Why should I let a bunch of smelly boys ruin my dinner? I'm going down and eat that chicken before Salem eats it all."

"That's the best idea I've heard all day," said Dreama.

The two teens walked back down the stairs, and before they reached the bottom, they heard Hilda yell, "You cat burglar! Get out of here!"

Salem ran in front of their path with a drumstick in his mouth. At once, Sabrina stumbled and fell, knocking Dreama off her feet. Both girls tumbled down the stairs and landed in a heap at the bottom.

"Ow," groaned Sabrina, rubbing a sore ankle. "What happened? Did you fall down?"

"No, *you* fell down," grumbled Dreama. "It was your fault."

"No, it wasn't," protested Sabrina. "I've walked down those stairs a million times—how could I fall down?"

"You're clumsy."

Sabrina scowled and staggered to her feet. "I am not clumsy!"

"Oh, yeah? I bet you couldn't walk under that ladder again without knocking it down."

"I bet I could!" Hobbling on her sore ankle, Sabrina went to the ladder and stepped under it. At once, the light fixture on the ceiling fell off and smashed on the top step of the ladder, showering Sabrina with bits of glass. She jumped out of the way and stared at the hole in the ceiling, shaking glass from her hair.

"Are you all right?" asked Dreama worriedly. "Someone as clumsy as you should be more careful."

"I am not clumsy!" insisted Sabrina. "I'm

going outside to do some exercises—I'll show you how graceful I am."

"Okay, go ahead."

Sabrina marched to the door and opened it. Outside in their front yard was a beautiful rainbow—with a large pot of gleaming cold coins resting at the bottom of it.

Sabrina's jaw dropped open. "Uh-oh."

"You forgot to turn off the rainbow," said Dreama. "Where did all that gold come from?"

"Hallelujah!" shouted a voice behind them. "My dreams have been answered!" Salem dashed outside, once again crossing their path. Immediately, the front door slammed shut behind them, and Sabrina heard an ominous click.

She tried the door and found it locked. She pointed her finger at the door and zapped it with magic, but it was still locked. "We're locked out," said Sabrina in amazement.

Dreama nodded. "See how clumsy you are."

"I think it's worse than that," answered Sabrina. "I think we're getting bad luck . . . as if superstitions are really working."

"But I just made them all worthless," insisted Dreama.

"Yes, so you did." Sabrina looked puzzledly at her fellow witch. "Unless something went wrong with your spell."

"I'm rich! I'm rich!" cackled Salem, rolling around in his pile of gold coins. "And I can give people bad luck. What a wonderful day!"

Sabrina and Dreama ran around to the back door of Sabrina's house, opened it, and rushed into the kitchen. There they found Aunt Hilda and Aunt Zelda eating their dinner at the kitchen table. They looked happy and contented, as if nothing were wrong in either realm.

Sabrina let out a sigh of relief, thinking that she must be going crazy. Still, she had to find out for sure. "Aunt Hilda, do you still have that wishbone?" she asked.

"Right here," said Hilda proudly. "You want to give it a little tug?"

"Yes, I do." Sabrina sat down at the table and rolled up her sleeves, as if she were going to arm wrestle.

"I thought you didn't believe in superstitions," said Aunt Zelda with amusement.

"Well, I may be changing my mind." Sabrina held out her hand with a determined look on her face. "Let's do it."

"Okay, but I warn you, I was wishbone-pulling champion in third grade." Hilda held out the wishbone, which was still a little gooey from being part of a freshly cooked chicken dinner. "We should let it dry out first."

"Please, can we just do it?" begged Sabrina.

"Okay." They each grabbed an end of the clavicle and pulled. After tugging on the soft wishbone for a while, Hilda finally snapped off the larger portion. "I win!"

All at once the telephone rang, and Zelda rose from the table to answer it. "Hello, Spellman residence." She listened thoughtfully for a moment. "You say that Hilda Spellman just won an all-expenses paid vacation to Hawaii? The tickets are in the mail? Thank you, I'll let her know."

"Yay!" shouted Hilda.

Zelda hung up and turned to Sabrina. "Okay, what's going on?"

Sabrina shook her head puzzledly. "I don't know how this could backfire, but Dreama just cast a spell that made all superstitions worthless."

Both Hilda and Zelda gasped out loud and looked horrified. Hilda put her hand to her mouth and turned to Dreama. "You cast a bad luck spell on the entire mortal population!"

"No, I didn't," protested Dreama. "I cast a 'no luck' spell."

"Don't you see," said Zelda, "making a good luck superstition fail is the same as casting bad luck. That's something a witch should never do—and you did it to every person on Earth. The results are catastrophic."

Sabrina groaned. "How do you define 'catastrophic'?"

"First," said Zelda, "the result of the spell will be the exact opposite, so now every crazy mortal superstition is absolutely real. For *everyone,* including witches. Second, all witches' magic will backfire, so whatever spell they cast, just the opposite will happen."

"Oh, no," muttered Dreama.

"It gets worse," said Hilda. "If the spell isn't broken in three days, the Witches' Council will turn you into a toad for a thousand years. They're probably already looking for you, Dreama."

"Can't we reverse the spell?" asked Sabrina.

Zelda shook her head. "No, because now all magic backfires. So to reverse the bad-luck spell, the bad-luck spell would have to be cast again. That would result in all the awful consequences starting all over again. It's a bewitched Catch-22."

Sabrina's face lit up with a ray of hope. "But Dreama's spells never last very long. So it will probably wear off!"

"But now just the opposite happens," answered Zelda, "so it will probably last forever."

Hilda rose from her seat and looked worriedly out the kitchen window. "If you thought mortals were superstitious before, wait until you see them now."

"I should go home," said Dreama worriedly.

"No, you should spend the night here," answered Zelda. "The Witches' Council will be looking for whoever did this. In fact, I don't think it's going to be safe for any of us to go outside."

"Yeah," said Hilda with a shudder. "What if I step on a crack? I'll break my mother's back!"

"Do you think it's going to be that bad?" asked Dreama.

"Let's put it this way," said Zelda, "you just gave all mortals the ability to work magic."

The four witches looked at one another in absolute horror.

Chapter 3

Drell, the powerful warlock who was head of the Witches' Council, looked puzzledly at himself. A few seconds ago, he had been sort of normal-looking, for a warlock, but now he had green skin, a wide mouth, and beady eyes on top of his head.

"Ribbit!" said Drell in alarm.

"Pardon me, your highness?" asked an assistant of his, Biff. "I thought you were going to turn the *prince* into a frog, not yourself."

"Ribbit!" answered Drell. He began hopping around frantically, and the prince who was supposed to be turned into a frog dashed from the council chambers.

Suddenly, there was a flash of light and a gust

of smoke, and Drell was himself again—except that he was sitting like a frog. The warlock jumped to his feet and wiped the dust off his silk pajamas.

"I just turned myself into a frog!" croaked Drell.

"I know you did," replied Biff. "And a very handsome frog, too, if I may say so."

"No, you nitwit! I just turned myself into a frog, and that's when I became human again. I became a frog when I tried to turn the *prince* into a frog." He scratched his head puzzledly. "I haven't had a spell backfire on me in five hundred years, and now it happens twice in a row!"

"Maybe you're losing your grip, sir." Biff smiled obsequiously. "Perhaps it's time to let *me* take over the Witches' Council."

Drell folded his arms and stared down at his pipsqueak assistant. "Something strange is going on here. Let's see *you* do some magic."

"Like what, sir?"

"Something simple." He looked around the luxurious furnishing of the council chamber. "Let's see you turn that vase of flowers into a porcupine."

"Do we really need a porcupine in here?" asked Biff. "They're so messy."

"Just do it."

Biff pointed a crooked finger at a lovely vase

of lilacs and daffodils. There was a flash of sparkling light, and the short warlock turned himself into a fat, spiny porcupine.

"Ah-ha!" bellowed Drell. "Do you still think there's nothing wrong?"

The porcupine didn't say anything—he just rooted under the cushions of the couch, looking for bugs. Drell strode across the room and punched a red button on his desk. At once, a loud siren sounded, whooping and wailing like a submarine making an emergency dive.

A few seconds later, an army of secretaries and sycophants rushed into the council chambers. They were armed with notebooks, laptop computers, and huge nets.

"We'll catch him, sir!" One of the men went after the porcupine with a net.

"No, don't worry about him," said Drell. "There's something really serious going on. I think all spells cast by any witch are going to backfire, and I don't know why. I don't like not knowing why."

The angry warlock began to pace the room. "This couldn't happen by accident. It's got to be caused by a witch casting a really dumb spell. I want a record of all spells cast in the last four hours."

"But, sir," protested one of the assistants, "that could be thousands of spells and thousands of witches! It will take a lot of work."

Drell glared at the man. "Would you like to be a porcupine, too?"

"No, your highness. I shall leave immediately." The man made a low bow, then he stood up and snapped his fingers. At once, he turned into a huge pile of leaves.

"Don't you people listen to me?" shouted Drell. "Don't use any magic, or it will backfire on you."

The others stood around, staring in shock at the pile of leaves that had once been their colleague. The porcupine instantly charged into the pile and scattered the leaves all over the room.

"Convene a meeting of the Witches' Council," ordered Drell. "No, don't do that. They'll use magic to get here, and who knows where they'll end up. I'll have to handle this myself."

"Should we put out an advisory to all witches?" asked a secretary.

"Good idea," answered Drell. "But don't use any magic! Call them up on mortal phones, write e-mail, or send letters."

"Oooh," moaned one woman. "If we have to use the post office, it really is bad."

Drell stalked across the room, pointing at people. "You and you, do the advisory. You two, capture the porcupine. The rest of you, get me those spell records."

"Yes, sir!" chimed his sycophants. They

rushed from the room, bumping into one another in their haste. Two of them cornered the porcupine and threw a net over him. The wild animal dragged them halfway across the room and stuck them with spines, but they finally managed to bring the beast before the president of the Witches' Council.

Drell knelt down and gazed into the porcupine's angry eyes. "Somewhere in that spiny carcass is my assistant, Biff. Listen to me, Biff—you have to try to cast a spell to turn yourself into a porcupine. I know this seems redundant, because you already *are* a porcupine; but this is the only way it will work."

A second later, it was Biff inside the net. The little warlock struggled to stand up. "Thank you for saving me, sir."

"I didn't do it for you," said Drell brusquely. "I need all the help I can get. But we're going to find out who did this awful thing, and when we do, we're going to squash them like a bug!"

"Mmmm," said Biff, licking his lips. "Bugs."

That night, Sabrina, Dreama, Hilda, and Zelda sat huddled around the television set, watching the news. They were in shock, because this was not the Mortal Realm they were used to.

A handsome newscaster smiled cheerfully and said, "Today's lottery numbers are 7, 13, 33, 44,

51, and 69. The jackpot is twenty-two million dollars, and since there are expected to be forty-four million winners, everyone will get fifty cents. Congratulations to all you winners. And if you didn't win, obviously you weren't playing."

He went on, "There was a terrible airplane crash over the Atlantic Ocean today, when a plane carrying two hundred people was torn apart by hurricane winds. No one was hurt, except for one small boy who opened an umbrella inside the plane."

"You have to watch out for those umbrellas," said his partner, a perky blond woman. "I don't even allow umbrellas inside my house."

"Me neither," agreed the newsman.

Instantly Hilda jumped to her feet.

"Where are you going?" asked Sabrina.

"To get rid of the umbrellas." She dashed out of the living room.

"In further news," continued the TV reporter, "there was a house fire on East Elm Street. Police say it was caused by somebody throwing his hat on the bed."

"Oh, this is terrible," muttered Dreama, burying her face in her hands. "I can't believe I did this to the world."

"It's like they don't even know what life was like before superstitions," said Sabrina in amazement.

"Isn't that just like the news," said Hilda, returning to the room. "Nothing but bad luck."

Somebody handed the newswoman a piece of paper. She read it, and the vacant smile vanished from her face. "Here's a late-breaking news story, and it's very serious. A *black cat* has been spotted inside the city limits. If you have any information regarding the whereabouts of this black cat, call the police immediately."

"I thought we got rid of all the black cats," said her partner with concern.

With a loud crash, the picture window smashed to bits as a dark object hurtled into the living room. Sabrina screamed and jumped to her feet. At first, she thought the object was a rock, until it slowly uncurled and revealed itself to be a black cat, covered in leaves and mud.

"Hide me, please!" begged Salem. "They're chasing me all over town!"

"Just don't cross my path," said Zelda. Gingerly, she bent down and picked up the cat, while someone pounded loudly on the front door.

Salem whimpered. "Don't let them get me!"

Sabrina rushed to the door, while Zelda spirited the cat into the kitchen. When the teenage witch opened the door, she was confronted by an angry mob.

A big man stepped forward. "Have you seen a black cat? We saw him coming this way."

"Uh, no," said Sabrina with a nervous laugh. "What would I be doing with a black cat?"

"How did your window get broken?" asked the man suspiciously.

"Oh, I . . . I walked under a ladder."

"That will do it every time," agreed the man. "If you see this black cat, don't mess around with it—call the police."

"Good advice," commented Sabrina. "Have a good-luck evening." With a relieved sigh, she shut the door and rushed to the window to make sure the crowd was leaving.

"Oh," said Hilda wistfully, "it's been a long time since I've seen an angry mob. It takes me back to my youth."

Sabrina pointed at the broken window, and the glass instantly reformed into one piece.

"How did you do that?" asked Dreama.

"I cast a spell to break it," answered Sabrina. "We can still do magic if we just remember to do everything in reverse."

Zelda returned from the kitchen, holding a shivering black cat. "I'm sorry, I'm sorry!" pleaded Salem. "It was so much fun to run in front of them and watch them fall down or crash their cars. How could I resist?"

"You had better learn to keep a low profile," warned Sabrina. She scratched her chin thoughtfully. "I wonder if I could turn you into a white kitty, like Dreama's."

"For a witch's familiar, I prefer basic black," said Salem. "If you want to do something, why don't you *reverse* this stupid spell? You haven't been outside yet. It's crazy! People are combing their yards for four-leaf clovers, chasing horses to get their shoes. The only thing worse to be right now than a black cat is a rabbit."

"We don't know what to do," answered Zelda, setting the cat on the floor. "All of our magic is reversed. So we would have to cast a bad-luck spell in order to counter Dreama's bad-luck spell, and that would make things worse."

Salem lowered his head and sobbed. "So I have to live in hiding for the rest of my life? I feel like a gangster who ratted on the mob."

"We're going to do *something*," answered Sabrina, pacing nervously. "We just don't know what."

"Maybe we should sleep on it," said Dreama with a yawn. "Things might look clearer in the morning."

Aunt Zelda nodded. "That's probably a good idea. You can stay in Sabrina's room."

"Just don't throw a hat on the bed," cautioned Aunt Hilda. "I like this house and don't want to see it burned down. Salem, you go to the kitchen, and walk around everybody. Walk along the walls, or on top of the furniture. You can do that, you're a cat."

"Maybe you could make me a gray cat, with black stripes," suggested Salem.

"I'm not going to do any magic on a living

being," said Sabrina. "We don't know how it would turn out. So stay out of sight."

The cat slunk away, sticking to the wall. He could be heard to sniffle. "I've never felt like such an outcast before."

Wearily Sabrina climbed the stairs. "Goodnight, everyone. Don't get up on the wrong side of the bed."

"I'm getting up on the *end* of my bed," Hilda assured her. "Hey, it's bad luck to cross somebody going different directions on the stairs, so we should all go up at the same time. Come on, Zelda."

When Sabrina reached the top of the stairs, she paused in front of the linen closet. Right behind her came Dreama, and she was so deep in worry that she bumped into Sabrina, pushing them both toward the linen closet. They stopped to gaze at the closet door, which beckoned so temptingly.

"I wonder if the closet is still a portal?" asked Sabrina curiously. "It might be safer for Salem over there."

"And for me," breathed Dreama. "I don't want to be a toad."

"Don't try it," warned Zelda, climbing right behind them. "Magical items are going to be really unpredictable."

"The closet probably won't take you anywhere," said Aunt Hilda, bringing up the rear.

"The opposite of going to the Other Realm is staying here."

"Or maybe the opposite is not existing at all," replied Aunt Zelda, "and you turn into a puff of dust."

"Aren't you the cheery one," sniffed Hilda. "You know, we could make the best of it, living in this new arrangement. So more people have magic? It might be fun winning the lottery every week. Maybe Dreama created a magical paradise!"

With exuberance, Aunt Hilda started forward and stepped on the shoelace of her tennis shoe, tripping herself. "Darn it." She bent down to tie the lace, gave it a tug, and it broke off in her hand. She looked up worriedly. "If I remember correctly, this is not good."

Bang! Bang! Bang! came loud pounding on the front door. Hilda peered down the stairs and hissed, "Shoot, the mob is back. Which one of us should handle this?"

"I answered it the first time," said Sabrina, taking a deep breath and marching down the stairs. Plastering a pleasant smile on her face, the teenage witch opened the door.

Once again, she was confronted by the big man in the plaid shirt and his mini-mob, which was smaller than before. "Someone saw that black cat running across your backyard," he said accusingly. His mob grumbled their disapproval.

"Well, maybe it was hiding under our house," answered Sabrina. "Are you sure this black cat ran off?"

"Yes, he ran off into the alley. Who knows how much misery he'll cause. He made me crack up my pickup truck." The big man's eyes blazed with anger, and Sabrina tried to counter him with sweetness.

"Well, I'm sure glad you big, strong cat hunters are looking out for us," cooed Sabrina. "If you hadn't scared that black cat away, he might have been lurking around our house for *days*. How can we ever thank you? Would you like some cold chicken?"

"No, thanks, I eat chicken three times a day," answered the man. "Collecting wishbones."

"I'm sure," said Sabrina, edging the door shut. "Good luck to you, finding that cat and all."

"We're watching you, missy," warned the man as the door shut in his face.

Sabrina let out a relieved sigh, then she rushed into the kitchen. "Salem! Salem!" she called. She checked the bathroom, the laundry room, all his usual haunts, but he was nowhere to be found. She discovered an open window in the laundry room, and his cat door was unlocked. He could have ducked outside either way.

Sabrina ran to the back door, threw it open, and stepped outside. She stared helplessly into the darkness as she shivered with the autumn cold, wondering if her pet was all right. Unable to use witchcraft, or even call out his name, Sabrina felt totally helpless. She knew the superstition vigilantes were out there somewhere, watching for Salem. Now that he was gone, he had to stay away.

With a tear in her eye, she whispered, "Take care of yourself, Salem."

Chapter 4

☆

☆

Drell was pacing the abandoned chamber of the Witches' Council, talking into a mortal cell phone. As he shouted into the phone, his voice echoed throughout the cavernous room. "Yes! Yes! I know how bad it is—I know we can't even use magic. Well, we *can* use it, but it backfires."

The warlock grimaced angrily. "No, we haven't caught the witch who did this yet. I've got people working on it, but it will take time to search the records. I've gotten reports from the Mortal Realm, and I hear it's loaded with magic over there. I can't figure out what happened. You tell the other council members not to worry, because we'll catch the traitor who did this. And when we do, we'll make an example of them."

The signal suddenly went dead, and Drell

shouted into the phone, "Hello? Hello?" He heard nothing except for a screech of static.

"Lousy mortal technology!" Drell hurled the cell phone into a huge fireplace, and it exploded in the flames with a loud pop. "Mortals don't need cell phones anymore—they've got more magic than *we* do!"

The great doors to the chamber creaked open, and little Biff rushed in, waving a piece of paper. "My Liege!" he shouted happily, "your staff has tracked down the idiot who cast that awful spell." He waved the paper in Drell's face.

"Let me see that." Drell snatched the paper from his assistant's hand and read it to himself. "I might have known. It's that young witch we sent to the Spellman household for training. Of course, the Spellmans corrupted her. We'll punish *all* of them!" he thundered.

"We have to catch them first," said Biff. "They're in the Mortal Realm, and the portals are dangerous to use."

"I know that." Drell paced for a moment, tapping his chin. "We'll send a posse of witch bounty hunters."

Biff shivered. "Is that really necessary, sir? They're rather . . . unpredictable."

"Right now, everything is unpredictable," muttered the warlock. "It's dangerous to change realms, but if we lose a few bounty hunters, no big deal."

"Of course, sir. Good thinking."

Drell stopped pacing and towered over his small assistant. "So what are you waiting for? Summon the bounty hunters!"

"Yes, Your Highness." Bowing obsequiously, the assistant backed out of the room.

Drell studied the piece of paper, musing aloud, "Where are you right now, Dreama? What are you doing? I can't use witchcraft to find you, but I can use my brain. What do I know about teenage girls?"

The great warlock paced some more, then he looked at his watch and nodded sagely to himself. "It's daytime in the Mortal Realm. I know where you'd be—the strangest place of all . . . high school."

The first bell rang, and Sabrina and Dreama walked cautiously up the main steps of Westbridge High School. Some kids were sitting on the lawn, combing through the grass, and Sabrina figured they were looking for four-leaf clovers. Probably had tests today. Otherwise, things appeared almost normal, with a mad rush of students trying to beat the second bell.

As they walked through the hallway, they noticed kids opening their lockers to get their books. Instead of the usual pictures of rock stars and actors hanging inside every locker there were horseshoes, rabbits' feet, four-leaf clovers, St.

Christopher medals, and dozens of personal good-luck charms. All the horseshoes were hung so that the open end pointed upward, so Sabrina figured that must be important.

"I'll get my books and meet you at your locker," said Dreama.

"Okay." Sabrina looked around, saying hello to several students she knew. One of them was wearing a string of garlic around his neck, and another was wearing a green hat covered in clovers.

She passed an animated conversation and caught a few words of it. "Did you hear about that black cat? It was actually *loose* on the streets—I saw it on TV."

"Oh, my gosh!" another student exclaimed in horror. "A black cat. Can you imagine?"

Sabrina sniffed, because she was more worried than ever about her poor black kitty. But Salem was resourceful and intelligent—he would find a way to survive. Wouldn't he?

She stopped at her locker, almost afraid to open it. But she had to go on with regular life until they figured out how to reverse the superstition spell. Holding her breath, Sabrina opened her locker.

She was quite relieved to find nothing inside, except for the usual mess—bits of papers, books, trash, a few pictures and notes. She didn't know why, but it seemed like a good idea to check her class schedule. So Sabrina opened up her favorite binder, which had her schedule in it.

A moment later, her jaw fell wide open, and she stared at the piece of paper. She didn't even hear Dreama come up behind her.

"Pretty spooky, huh?" asked Dreama.

Flopping her mouth open like a fish, Sabrina pointed at the printed schedule. "Look . . . look at this! For first period, I have Horseshoes 101."

Dreama pointed at Sabrina's schedule. "Hey, we have a class together, taught by Mrs. Quick— Advanced Augury. What's *augury?* It's not as bad as trigonometry, is it?"

"It's worse," whispered Sabrina. "That's when mortals used to think they could tell the future by looking at animal bones and guts. Girl, you sent us back into the Dark Ages!"

"Well, I'm sorry, I didn't mean—" Before Dreama could finish her sentence, her eyes widened, and she stared past Sabrina down the corridor. "Uh, speaking of the Dark Ages . . ."

Sabrina whirled around just as the front doors opened, and a gang of dirty hulks marched in. They were covered with soot and dirt, as if they were mine workers; but they also wore grimy pads and helmets, like football players.

Other students shrunk away from the bums, some holding their noses or gagging, others afraid. The gang strutted toward Sabrina as if they owned the school, but she didn't recognize them until their putrid smell reached her nose.

Sabrina gasped. "It's the football players!"

"No!" exclaimed Dreama in disbelief.

"Yes, it is. Look!"

Sure enough, under the grimy, oily uniforms were the familiar faces of Harvey, Brad, Billy, and the rest of the football players. They walked with a real swagger now, as if they were too cool for anyone else, but it was their smell that was the most impressive. They reeked even worse than before.

Harvey sauntered straight toward Sabrina, his lip curling into a smile. "Hiya, Babe. Give your old man a kiss."

Sabrina had nowhere to run, nowhere to hide. All she could do was hold her breath and try not to gag as Harvey planted a wet one on her. Surrounded by smelly football players, she nearly fainted.

"Hey, big game this weekend," said Harvey. "You going to be there?"

"But of course," she answered hoarsely.

"Not that it makes much difference," said Harvey. "We win all of our games, anyway."

Brad stepped close to Harvey. "Better knock on wood after you say that."

"No problem. Come here, Petey!" Harvey motioned to one of the other players, and he rushed over. With amazement, Sabrina noted that his helmet was really a wooden salad bowl. Harvey gave the wooden bowl several good knocks, then he smiled cheerfully at his girlfriend.

"Our no-bathing, no-changing-clothes policy is working so well that Coach says we don't even have to practice anymore." Harvey grinned.

"How fortunate for you," said Sabrina. "But they let you wear your uniform all day in school?"

"Mr. Kraft wouldn't have it any other way." Harvey looked around the crowded hallway. "Where is our beloved principal?"

"He accidentally broke a spider's web," answered Brad. "Now he's afraid to come out of his office."

"I would be, too," said Harvey, shivering at the thought of it. He cuffed Sabrina on the chin. "I'll see you later, Babe. I couldn't find any clovers this morning, so I have to study for a test."

"Well, good luck," said Sabrina cheerfully.

"Always."

Harvey walked on, but Brad passed Sabrina and looked puzzledly at her. "There's something different about you today."

Sabrina gave a nervous laugh. "Oh, yeah? Like what?"

"I always thought you were kind of weird," answered Brad. "But you don't seem so weird today."

"Not compared to all of you," blurted Sabrina.

Brad looked suspiciously at her. "Are you cutting on us? We've got the best superstition in school working for us."

"It's impressive," agreed Sabrina, trying not to hold her nose. "I'm sure you'll win, and I'll be rooting for you."

"You're okay," said Brad, giving her half a smile. He sauntered off with this buddies, and Sabrina turned to Dreama.

"I've never seen him so friendly to you before," observed Dreama.

Sabrina nodded thoughtfully. "It's weird, but now that Brad has his own magic, maybe he can't sense ours. Or maybe—since our magic is reversed—I'm sending out some kind of reversed vibes. When he sees me now, he's sure I'm totally mundane."

"I guess there's always a silver lining," said Dreama. "Or is that a superstition?"

The second bell rang, and Dreama and Sabrina looked worriedly at one another. "I'll keep an eye out for you," promised Sabrina. "I know I tell you not to do magic at school, but *really* don't do it."

"Okay." Dreama crossed her fingers. "I'm new at this, but I wish you luck."

"You, too."

Sabrina could hardly believe her eyes: Mrs. Pritchard's classroom had been turned into a blacksmith shop! There was a smoldering fire in the furnace, kept alive by a giant bellows. Horseshoes, iron strips, and primitive tools hung from hooks in the ceiling, and an anvil stood in the center of the room. All they lacked was a horse.

While she gaped around, Sabrina kicked something on the floor, and she looked down to see a horseshoe nail. She was about to step over it, when the boy behind her gasped.

"Aren't you going to pick that up?" he asked, pointing to the nail. "Can I have it?"

"No!" said Sabrina quickly. She bent down to scoop up the horseshoe nail, needing as much good luck as she could get.

Good luck didn't come right away, because she turned and saw Mr. Kraft sitting at the teacher's desk. The principal held a rabbit's foot in one hand and frantically stroked it with the other. He smiled nervously at the students as they filed in, and he looked especially nervous when he saw Sabrina.

"Miss Spellman, sit in the back!" he ordered. "I've already had one bad-luck incident today, and I don't need *you* jinxing me."

"Yes, sir," answered Sabrina, anxious to get to the back, away from the jumpy principal. Being a slave to superstitions had turned Mr. Kraft into a nervous wreck.

"Good morning, class." Mr. Kraft rose to his feet and mustered some of his old bravado. But he still gripped his rabbit's foot behind his back.

"I had a bit of bad luck this morning, so I thought I would redeem myself by teaching the horseshoe class. What is more comforting than being surrounded by horseshoes? I've given Mrs. Pritchard the day off—to find a toad in her basement."

The students all looked at one other as if this were a worthy reason, and Sabrina sunk deeper into her seat.

"First of all, I have a special surprise," said Mr. Kraft, beaming. "I dropped a horseshoe nail on the floor. This was a very special nail—it had actually been worn by a horse!"

An excited buzz circulated around the class, and Kraft went on, "I'm sure one of you picked up that nail. Come on, don't be bashful—who was it?"

The boy from the door whirled and pointed at Sabrina. "It was Sabrina! She picked it up."

All eyes turned her way, drilling into the embarrassed teenager, who edged behind the bellows at the rear of the blacksmith shop. They smiled expectantly, as if she were queen of the class.

"Ah, Miss Spellman," said Kraft pleasantly. "I thought you had a certain glow about you today. You don't mind if I stand beside you, do you?"

"No," answered Sabrina, felling very silly, even though finding the nail was a good thing. She held up the iron prize, amazed at all the fuss.

"Put it in your pocket," warned Mr. Kraft. "Don't carry it anywhere but your pocket."

"If you say so." Sabrina quickly pocketed the horseshoe nail, and the rest of the class finally looked away.

But Mr. Kraft stood very close beside her. "All right, class, let's see how much you know. If you find a horseshoe, what's the best way to get good luck out of it?"

Eager hands shot into the air, and Mr. Kraft had his pick. He glanced at Sabrina to see if she wanted to answer, but she slumped deeper into her seat.

"Okay, Miss Collins, what's your answer?"

Jessica, a brainy kid who always got the right answer, jumped to her feet. "You spit on it and throw it away, tossing it over your left shoulder."

"Very good," answered Mr. Kraft. "This also spreads the good luck around." The students looked happily at one another, as if this bit of knowledge had made their day.

Mr. Kraft wagged his finger at the students. "You must be careful not to confuse a horseshoe with a muleshoe, as muleshoes are bad luck."

Sabrina couldn't take it any longer, and she laughed out loud. Mr. Kraft gazed sternly at her. "And what is so funny, Miss Spellman?"

"Well, you don't see many horses around here," she explained, "and I don't know when I last saw a *mule*."

Kraft waved to one of the students seated against the row of windows. "Open up those blinds, Mr. Habib."

The boy jumped to his feet and opened the thick blinds that shielded the windows. At once, the sun streamed into the smithy, and so did a bucolic scene of horses and mules, standing in a corral outside. Sabrina jumped up from her desk, unable to believe her eyes. The entire schoolyard had been turned into a farmyard.

She pointed at the bizarre scene. "That . . . that wasn't there—"

"When wasn't it there?" asked Kraft. "We've had a laboratory for horseshoes at this school ever since I can remember. Who can tell me the most common use for horsehair?"

A lot of hands shot up, and he pointed at Jessica again. She stood up and said smugly, "You rub horsehair on a baby's stomach to cure whooping cough!"

"Absolutely, right." He looked disapprovingly at Sabrina. "How could you not know that?"

"I think I was sick during whooping cough." Sabrina tried to shrink so far into her seat that she would be invisible. *This is going to be a long day,* she thought to herself. *I wonder how Salem is getting along?*

Chapter 5

The black cat darted under a fence gate just as a pitchfork came flying through the air, missing him by a hair. He scooted under the fence before a large rock crashed into the wood.

"Get that cat!" came a shout.

"Don't let him escape!" cried another person.

Huffing and puffing, Salem tore across the field, trying to keep low in the plowed furrows. But it was mid-autumn, and nothing was growing; he didn't have much cover. A cry rang out, and the cat glanced back to see the mob jumping over the fence. Hollering and shaking their fists, the crowd bounded across the field.

A group of swift runners was catching up. Some of them were holding a net! If he didn't do something fast, they'd get him for sure.

Suddenly Salem remembered something: *I have weapons at my disposal—I am an offensive powerhouse!* He tried to think back to the days when he was a warlock and could unleash dreadful spells on everybody. *I have to get tough and ruthless,* he told himself. *I'll show them!*

The cat made a wide turn and looped around, heading back toward his pursuers. He wasn't going to attack them; his plan was to cross in front of them! The crowd slowed, realizing in a panic that bad luck was headed their way.

A couple of the braver ones began to follow him again, so he concentrated on them. Running as fast as his furry legs could take him, Salem dashed to cut off his pursuers. It turned into a mad race, with both the cat and the people running in crazy zigzags to outmaneuver their foe.

Hah! Salem made a sharp cut and dashed behind the men, running a circle around them. Now no matter which way they went, bad luck would befall them! One of his pursuers skidded to a stop in time, but the other one stumbled and rolled head-over-heels across the invisible line of chaos.

Salem saw the man's car keys fall out of his pocket, although he jumped up without noticing. The cat didn't wait around to see what happened next—he made a bee line for the tree line. Before the mob realized it, their prey was gone.

They whooped and hollered, and threw things. "Good riddance to bad luck!" bellowed one guy. Another one shouted, "I hope you run under a ladder!"

The bedraggled cat kept running until he reached the cover of the forest, then he crawled under a bush and collapsed. His chest heaving, Salem lay still for several moments, listening to see if anyone was chasing after him. He heard the people muttering and tromping around the field, but they didn't seem to be coming into the forest.

Whew! he thought. *I escaped the mob this time, but next time the pitchforks might get me. I'm hungry, thirsty, dirty, and exhausted, but I can't go home. What am I going to do?*

Salem looked down at his matted black fur, knowing that he needed some kind of disguise. But what? They didn't have makeup for cats. And even if he found a costume that fit him, he would still be a cat in a costume.

He noticed there were berries on the bush over his head, and he gave them a sniff. They didn't smell poisonous. Salem could feel his animal instincts starting to take over, and he had to trust those instincts. That was all he had. So he ate a few berries off the bush.

Salem held his breath, waiting to die, but nothing happened. *Maybe I can survive out here, but for how long?* He knew he had to keep moving, because those people might be back. So Salem crawled off through the woods, keeping under-cover.

As he moved along, he tried to think of cos-tumes that were practical and easy, but he couldn't really come up with any—until a certain odor caught his nostrils. Normally Salem didn't follow awful smells, but this one was so familiar that it again stirred his animal senses.

Salem inched warily toward the smell, careful not to get too close. The odor was like reeking cheese—limburger—mixed with a dirty diaper. He had a feeling he knew what it was.

The first visual sign was a plump black tail bouncing above the underbrush. Salem stopped, knowing he was already too close. He peered around a tree trunk and saw a furry black animal waddle into a clearing. The beast wasn't much larger than a cat, thought Salem. In fact, he could *be* a cat, except for that white stripe on his back . . . and his distinct odor.

Why had the skunk sprayed? wondered Salem. It must have been all the noise from the mob, be-cause there wasn't anyone else around. *That stink may be keeping those people away,* thought Salem. *Hmmmm.*

"Thank you, Mr. Skunk," whispered the cat. "You've given me an idea for a disguise. All I need is some white paint, and a really bad smell. Smelling bad should be no problem—not with *you* around." Salem knew what he had to do.

He took a deep breath and mustered his courage. Then he charged from his hiding place, crashing through the bushes. Just as the skunk whirled around, Salem leaped through the air. He howled like a mountain lion, but the skunk didn't seem too scared. He blasted Salem with a cloud of putrid musk anyway, and Salem fell to the ground, coughing and gagging.

His eyes and lungs burning, the cat looked up in a daze. He saw the skunk sniff the air, admiring his handiwork, then waddle off, in no hurry. The reeking odor hung in the air and clung to the cat like a jacket.

"Well, now I smell like a skunk," said Salem with satisfaction. "I've been accused of that before, but it's never been so true. I'm halfway there—now I just need to find some old white paint."

Stinking like a skunk, the cat padded through the forest, headed back toward the fence and the farms on the other side of it.

"These are fake wishbones, of course," said Mrs. Quick. "Real ones are much too valuable to hand out." The pinch-faced teacher walked down the aisle with a box, handing every student in her class a cheap plastic wishbone. The other students stared at them with interest, while Sabrina and Dreama just stared at each other.

Even Mrs. Quick is a superstition addict! thought Sabrina in alarm. *No one can escape superstitions in this wacky realm.*

"Now, students," said the teacher, "I don't need to tell you what you already know: You can't get anywhere in life if you don't know how to pull a wishbone. All the education in the world won't make any difference if your little sister always bests you. She'll be the one getting the money in your parents' will."

Mrs. Quick smiled thoughtfully. "Of course, we'll cover other kinds of augury: How to invest in the stock market by poking through sheep entrails. How to read squished bugs on the windshield, and many more topics. But nothing tells us more about the future than the wishbone."

She turned and looked directly at Sabrina. "Miss Spellman, should you grab high or low on the wishbone?"

Sabrina thought about that for a moment, then remembered how her Aunt Hilda did it. "High."

"Very good." Mrs. Quick beamed at her. "I heard you found a horseshoe nail today. Excellent work! Maybe there's a future for you yet."

Sabrina gulped. "I hope so."

"Find a partner," ordered the teacher. "Today we're going to practice the grip and technique of the common wishbone pull. We'll get fancier next quarter. The objective is to make a nice, even pull. Not too hard, or you risk causing a stress fracture and giving that wish to someone else."

Sabrina tugged on her fake wishbone and looked helplessly at Dreama, who rolled her eyes in disbelief. *Both of us have the same wish,* thought the teenage witch. *We wish that the anti-superstition spell had never happened.*

With a hammer, Aunt Hilda pounded the piece of paper onto a telephone pole near their street. It was a reward poster with a picture of Salem, their phone number, and the words: "Lost—black cat named Salem. Reward offered. No questions asked."

"That will never work," said Zelda. "People will think we're crazy for wanting a black cat. In this place, you don't have a black cat for a pet."

"Hmmm," said Hilda thoughtfully. "Okay, I'll change it." She took out a black marker and added words to the poster until it said: "Wanted—black cat criminal named Salem. Reward offered. Handle with care."

Hilda nodded, satisfied with her work. "If anyone asks, we'll say we're bounty hunters."

Zelda frowned and looked around the sunny street, which was strangely devoid of people and traffic. Word had gotten out that a black cat was on the prowl, and people were nervous.

"Let's go home," said Zelda worriedly. "I wish we could do a finder spell, but that's too risky."

Hilda pointed proudly to her feet. "Look, I put new pennies in my penny loafers. And they're pennies I found in the street, so that's double good luck! And the newspaper had a good tip today: Boiling two pennies in vinegar will cure a sprained ankle."

"Home," said Zelda, turning her sister around and pushing her down the sidewalk. "There's too much wild magic flying around here—I can feel it. Dreama really put a whammy on things."

"She thought she was helping," said Hilda. "Okay, we'll go home—maybe Salem has come back."

Zelda didn't say anything, because she knew how unlikely that was. If they ever saw their familiar again, it would be a miracle. All they could hope to do was find some way to set things straight before Dreama got punished. Then again, maybe this superstitious realm could never be reversed, and they would all have to learn new rules just to live.

The two witches hurried down the street. They passed no one, but they saw window drapes part as their neighbors cautiously watched them. Mortals now had magic, but at a terrible price— the constant and real fear of getting hit with bad luck. The good luck they'd found was hardly worth the trade-off.

They finally arrived home, and Zelda pushed the front door open with relief. She stepped in side, and her shoe crushed a bit of glass on the floor, which surprised her. Zelda stepped around the unexpected mess, as Hilda barged right past her.

Hilda skidded to a stop and shrieked, "What happened?"

Now Zelda took in the whole room, and she was equally shocked, although not surprised. The house had been turned upside-down, with papers scattered everywhere, drawers pulled out and dumped, chairs overturned, and cushions ripped up. Lamps had been ripped out of their sockets, and she had stepped on a broken light bulb.

"Well, this is too much!" shouted Hilda angrily. She began to roll up her sleeves. "If those hooligans think a black cat is bad luck, wait until they get a load of *me!*"

"No, no, don't lose your temper," warned Zelda, stepping cautiously into the room. "Another reversed spell could make things a lot worse. We don't know who did this, or what they were looking for. Maybe we crossed each other on the stairs, or broke some other silly superstition."

"It was those cat chasers," grumbled Hilda. "This isn't bad luck—it's dumbness. I don't know whether to go upstairs or to the kitchen. Which don't I want to see first?"

"Let's check upstairs and see if Salem's hiding up there." Zelda gulped. "Or if anyone else is up there."

Zelda bravely led the way up the stairs, while Hilda followed, muttering to herself. "If they've touched my clock collection, I'll brain them!"

When they reached the landing on the second floor, they found another mess. Clothes were strewn all over the hall, drawers were splintered into pieces, and there was even a hole in the wall, surrounded by burned plaster.

"I don't get it," said Hilda. "It looks like World War III."

Zelda shook her head puzzledly. "This doesn't look like something the mob would do while looking for a cat." She glanced around, and her eyes hit upon another small change.

"Did you leave the door to the linen closet open?" asked Zelda.

"No, I haven't had the courage to use it. If it's open, then somebody else must have used it."

Both witches turned to look at the open door. Inside the linen closet, the towels, washcloths, and sheets were perfectly stacked as usual. They weren't disturbed at all. "Whoever opened this door was careful not to mess it up," said Zelda. "They weren't looking in the closet."

"Then they were coming *out* of the closet," said Hilda. "We've had rude visitors from the Other Realm before, but this is ridiculous."

Zelda's eyes widened in shocked realization. "They weren't looking for Salem—they were looking for Dreama, Sabrina . . . *us!*"

"A posse of witch bounty hunters!" shouted Hilda. "Oh, my gosh, if they're not here, where have they gone?" The witches crouched down like commandos and surveyed the messy hallway, but all Zelda noticed was a chilly draft coming from the hole in the wall.

"Get out of the draft," said Hilda, pulling Zelda aside. "We'll catch a cold."

"That's just another crazy superstition!" yelled Zelda, exploding with pent-up anger. "Drafts don't cause colds—*viruses cause colds!* I want to get back to a world that makes just a little bit of sense, and this isn't it. In this Superstition Realm you can't even turn the magic off!"

Zelda paced across the carpet, pounding her hand into her fist. "The girls are in trouble, Salem is missing and presumed lost, a posse is after us, and I'm tired of getting superstitions rammed down my throat. I say it's time to fight back!"

"Okay," said Hilda, rushing for the stairs. "I'll be out in the yard, looking for four-leaf clovers."

Chapter 6

Sabrina looked around the girls' bathroom, hardly believing her eyes. All the mirrors were covered with thick boards—she guessed it was to keep them from breaking. Slivers of mirror were visible in the cracks between the boards, and girls bobbed back and forth, trying to see enough of themselves to brush their hair. It was a hopeless task, and most of the girls had half-combed hair.

"I think I'm going to get Danny Johnson to ask me out tonight," bragged Connie. "I found a pin today, and I put it on my pillow."

"You'll probably just poke your eye out," muttered Sabrina.

The girl turned on Sabrina. "What is that cut supposed to mean? I don't know what kind of

63

luck you use to hang on to Harvey, but you'd better watch out—I know some girls who have been saving up their clovers."

"I don't use any magic to hang onto Harvey. Er . . . I mean, luck." Sabrina pretended to peer into a boarded-up mirror, ignoring the other girls. There was no point trying to talk sense into them. With their crazy form of magic, mortals had become lazy and greedy. When they weren't obsessing over good luck, they were trying to avoid bad luck.

Sabrina dashed out of the bathroom to go to her next class, biology. That was usually a hard class for her, but the subject was at least rooted in reality. She entered the classroom just as the bell rang, and she quickly found a seat. When she looked around, Sabrina felt a great sense of relief, because this looked like a classroom.

The walls were covered with the usual posters of dissected frogs, people with their muscles exposed, and boring genetic charts about green beans. Instead of being gross, these peculiar objects were oddly reassuring today; they even seemed normal in this mixed-up world.

Sabrina was relieved to get back into a real class, imparting real information. Mr. Romero was a tough teacher, but he knew his stuff. He was a man of science—he wouldn't brook any of this superstitious nonsense. When the teacher entered the classroom a moment later, Sabrina folded her hands and sat straight in her seat, ready to learn.

"Good morning, class," said Mr. Romero with a beaming smile. "Guess what? Today we're going to have a pop quiz!"

Groans echoed around the classroom, and Sabrina smiled to herself. That reaction seemed perfectly normal. "Sorry I have to do a pop quiz," explained the teacher, "but it's the only way to avoid the four-leaf clovers, rabbits' feet, and other charms you kids lug around all day. I really want to see what you've learned about *biology* this quarter."

Sabrina felt for the horseshoe nail in her pocket, then laughed at herself. She didn't need a good-luck charm to ace a biology test. Well, maybe she did, but she wasn't going to depend on it.

Mr. Romero took a sheaf of papers from his desk drawer and walked down the aisle, handing them out. "I feel pretty lucky today," he said jokingly. "So maybe some of you will get less than an A. As soon as you have your test, you may begin."

Sabrina straightened her test paper and took a deep breath, because Mr. Romero was famous for his hard tests. With trepidation, she read the first question from the corner of her eye. The question was multiple choice, and it read:

1. *Sunstroke is a very serious health condition. You can avoid sunstroke by:*

A. lining your hat with oak leaves
B. carrying a potato in your traveling bag
C. placing cabbage leaves on your head
D. all of the above

Sabrina groaned and leaned back in her chair. This biology class wasn't going to be any better than any of the other classes! In this crazy realm, science had been replaced by superstitions and old wives' tales. She looked at the second question and was surprised that she actually knew the answer to it:

2. You can cure a black eye by:
   A. spitting on it
   B. placing a raw steak over the eye
   C. smearing vinegar and salt on the eyebrow
   D. all of the above

Sabrina wanted to scream. Shaking her head at the absurdity, she circled B, "Placing a raw steak over the eye." When had she learned that? How had all these crazy superstitions gotten started?

It must have been like the football players deciding not to bathe anymore, she thought. When a superstition worked out fine once or twice, why not keep doing it? Hundreds of years ago, some idiot had put a steak on his black eye, and it felt better; so now they all had to do it.

Suddenly there was a smashing sound, followed by shouts and commotion in the hallway. The scribbling of pencils stopped, and most of the class swiveled in their chairs to face the door. A few of them pulled out their rabbits' feet.

The door flew open, and six grizzled cowboys in chaps and floppy hats tried to charge through the door at once. All of them were spinning lassoes over their heads, and the ropes got tangled up together. The cowboys stumbled, their hats flew off, their spurs spun out, and they landed in a heap just inside the door.

One cowboy with a big moustache popped up from the pile and looked straight at Sabrina. "Thar she is, boys!"

That was Sabrina's cue to jump to her feet and look for an escape route. But there wasn't one, except for the door they were blocking.

"Sabrina Spellman!" intoned a gray-haired cowboy, staggering to his feet. "You are wanted for questioning by . . . you know who. We're a duly appointed posse, charged with bringing you in. Ready, boys?"

The cowboys scrambled to their feet and spread out around the room, whirling the lassoes over their heads as if they were going to catch a bunch of cattle. *I've got to warn Dreama,* thought Sabrina in alarm, *not to mention that I've got to get out of here!*

The witch pointed her finger and cast a hurried spell: "I would hate to be a mouse; make me as big as a house!"

She closed her eyes just as a lasso sailed through the air and settled around her shoulders. But when the cowboy yanked on his rope to reel her in, Sabrina's body disappeared in a twinkle of light.

Actually Sabrina hadn't disappeared—she shrank to a height of about two inches, no bigger than a mouse. As the posse fanned out around the room, tiny Sabrina shot between two huge feet and pressed up against a chair leg, which to her seemed as big as a tree trunk.

She tried to hide, but it was bedlam inside the classroom, with students and bounty hunters running everywhere, bumping into one another. The chair she was hiding behind got tipped over, and Sabrina had to dive out of the way to keep from being crushed.

When she looked up, she found herself in the middle of the floor, dodging huge cowboy boots and athletic shoes. Sabrina looked for somebody who was standing still, and she spotted the gray-suited leg of her teacher, Mr. Romero. He was the only one in the crowd wearing dress shoes.

She dashed toward his leg and jumped onto the back of his pant leg, hanging on like a mountain climber on a rope. Mr. Romero's pants were old-fashioned and had cuffs, and she noticed that his cuffs were open at the top. When the teacher suddenly moved, Sabrina almost lost her grip and nearly fell off. She knew she had to do something to help her hang on.

She quickly crawled into his pants cuff and hunkered down. When Mr. Romero began to walk, Sabrina swayed back and forth like a sailor in a hammock during a rough storm. The teacher only went a few steps before she feared she would be seasick.

"You people get out of here!" bellowed Mr. Romero, stomping angrily around the room. "Halloween is over!"

"They're cowboys," said a student. "Maybe they're looking for the blacksmith class."

Their leader, the man with the black moustache, pointed to the door. "Let's get the other one before she gets away. *Vamos!*"

Sabrina took a gulp of dusty air and peeped over the edge of the thick pants cuff. It was about an inch wide, and she was no more than twice that. She could see the cowboys stumbling out the door, their wide lassoes getting in the way.

She thought the worst was over until Mr. Romera followed them out, bouncing angrily on his feet. "Take your cowboy business down the hall! That's where the blacksmith is."

Their leader whirled around and tipped his hat.

"Thank you kindly, we'll check out that smithy. Come on, boys."

Sabrina wracked her brain, trying to remember where Dreama would be during this period. But Dreama was never too certain of her schedule, so she didn't talk about it much. If Dreama got captured now, she would be turned into a toad before they even had a chance to reverse the spell. They still had two more days, and they needed Dreama more than the Witches' Council needed her.

Once the posses left, the corridor seemed to be empty. Mr. Romero huffed and puffed but finally started back into his classroom. So Sabrina bailed out, leaping to the floor. She heard a door open, and she curled into a ball, hoping to look like one of the dust balls littering the corridor.

"Are you all right, Mr. Romero?" asked Mr. Kraft. The principal had just come out of a broom closet across the hall. What was he doing in the broom closet? wondered Sabrina. Maybe he was hiding—his clothes looked kind of rumpled.

"There was a commotion—some yahoos dressed like cowboys," said Mr. Romero. "I think they wanted the horseshoe class down the hall."

"No problem," said Mr. Kraft, looking nervous about everything. "I took all the horseshoes out of the class and put them' in my office . . . for safe keeping. Something tells me there's bad luck running rampant in these halls today."

"Yes, I heard about you and that spider web this morning," said Mr. Romero with a grimace. "Bad business."

Mr. Kraft sniffed sadly. "Thanks for your concern, but I think I've gotten over it. Just be a little more on guard than usual—I'll check on those intruders."

"Very good, sir." Romero turned smartly and stepped back into his classroom, then he remembered something and stuck his head out. "Sabrina Spellman seems to be missing. I didn't see her leave, but maybe she left with those cowboys. They seemed to know her."

Kraft twitched nervously. "I'm not suprised that Miss Spellman is involved. I'm sure that's where my premonition of trouble comes from. I'll find her!" He strode determinedly down the corridor, right past Sabrina, who was crouched behind a dust ball.

When the principal was gone, Sabrina jumped to her feet and ran for the stairwell. She ducked under the stairs, where the dust was as thick as a field of grass. This wasn't a very good hiding place, but at least she wasn't out in the open. It would take sharp eyes to spot her, but she didn't want to take any chances.

If Mr. Kraft was out wandering around, then his office had to be empty, she reasoned. She could look up Dreama's schedule on his computer, if she could figure out a way to work it.

Sabrina thought about trying to cast another reverse spell to return to her normal size, but she had been lucky with that other spell. Besides, it might be easier to sneak around the school in this mini size.

Sticking to the wall for cover, Sabrina rushed down the hallway, jumping over bits of garbage and gum wrappers. With such short legs, it would take her forever to get to the office, but she had to do something.

"Boy, I wish this had never happened," muttered Sabrina, panting hard as she ran.

Salem crouched in the bushes, about thirty feet away from two house painters, who were working on a large house. At the moment, they were high up on ladders, painting the second story of the house. Best of all, they were using white paint. On a board stretched between the ladders, they had buckets and rollers just full of dripping paint.

The black cat snickered to himself, thinking that two guys who worked around ladders had to be very superstitious. It wouldn't take much to spook them, although he had to be careful not to attract any bad luck to himself. *Maybe black cats are immune to bad luck,* thought Salem. *Still, I don't want to risk getting under those ladders.*

Or maybe I do.

"Hey, Mike," said the taller of the two painters, "I think it's about time for lunch, isn't it?"

"Yeah, just let me finish this spot." The shorter painter stood on his tiptoes to reach a high spot with his paint roller. "Okay, I'm ready."

Uh-oh, thought Salem, *I'll have to work fast*. He dashed from his hiding place under the bushes and ran across the front yard. Throwing caution to the wind, he crossed between the ladders and stood underneath them. Not really under them, but close enough to be nervous.

"Hi, boys," he said to the painters. "You're doing a great job there."

They were so shocked by his sudden appearance that both of them nearly fell off their ladders. "John, l-look at that!" sputtered the short one. "It's a black cat!"

"A *talking* black cat," said John with a shudder.

"That's right," agreed Salem, "and if you know anything about black cats, you know what I can do to you. Now I want you to poor out some white paint on the ground and do it very slowly."

"Here, you can have the whole bucket!" shouted Mike. He grabbed his paint bucket and hurled it at the black cat.

The bucket hit the ground hard, splattering paint everywhere. Instinctively, the cat jumped to his left to avoid the bucket, and he found himself right under John's ladder. The painter shouted in alarm and leaned too far back—his ladder started to tip away from the house.

"Help!" he shouted, but it was too late. John fell back into the tree behind him, pulling the board and the other ladder down with him.

"Whoa!" screamed Mike, his hands wind-milling as he fell. Salem looked up to see paint buckets, rollers, and brushes plummeting toward him, and he quickly curled into a ball.

Like gooey bombs, the cans of white paint exploded all around the cat, and he hunkered down, trying to expose just his back. It worked, as a stream of cold, gooey paint coated his fur. "Ah," said Salem, "that feels good."

When the shouting finally stopped, Salem looked up to see one painter stuck in a tree and the other one lying on the roof of his pickup truck. The one on the truck jumped off and landed on the ground, looking wobbly on his feet.

Salem decided to try out his new disguise, so he strolled past the painter and stopped to look at him.

"Whaaa!" shrieked the man, jumping backwards and wrinkling his nose. "First a black cat, and now a *skunk!*" He sniffed his clothes and grimaced. "I guess I know what *my* bad luck will be."

"Mike!" yelled the one in the tree. "Help me!"

"Okay, but you won't want to get close to me."

While the two painters recovered from their run of bad luck, Salem sauntered boldly down the sidewalk. Although being a black cat was fun, being a skunk was safer, he decided. People ran in the opposite direction, and they never tried to catch him. Bad smell outruled bad luck.

Now that it's safe, it's time to go home, thought Salem as he pranced.

Chapter 7

Aunt Hilda stood outside the linen closet, staring into the open door. She was wearing safety goggles and an apron. She motioned with her hand as she shouted, "Okay, let it go!"

Standing behind her, Aunt Zelda gripped a pillow from the couch, and she made an exaggerated wind-up like a softball pitcher. With a grunt, she threw the pillow through the open door. It did nothing but sail to the back of the closet and bounce off the shelves.

"Hmmm," said Hilda, making a note on a pad of paper. "Experiment sixty-two has the same result—nothing. Maybe it's time to use a real witch."

"The portal hasn't worked right sixty-two times," said Zelda, "and you want one of *us* to try it?"

"Not you or me," answered Hilda with a nervous laugh. "I said a real witch, but I was thinking about the one who got us into this mess, Dreama."

"I wish Dreama were here," said Zelda worriedly, "and Sabrina, too. We could go down to school and look for them."

Hilda shook her head. "No, I think you had the right idea—to reach Drell and beg for some extra time. Only he can call off the bounty hunters."

Zelda frowned worriedly. "What if it's too late? What if we can't reverse the spell?"

"Then we'll go back to hunting four-leaf clovers." Hilda walked into Sabrina's room and looked out the window. "I wonder if there's any junk in the backyard that we can throw in there to test?"

Zelda peered into the apparently normal linen closet. "What I don't understand is why the bounty hunters got through and we can't?"

"Eeek!" shrieked Hilda.

Zelda ran into Sabrina's bedroom and rushed to her sister's side. "What's the matter?"

"There's a skunk in our backyard!" She pointed down at a black animal with a white stripe on its back. It was prancing across their backyard as if it owned the place.

"Ewww," said Zelda, wrinkling her nose. She watched with disgust as the smelly creature started to sniff around the back door. "He looks like he's trying to get into the house!"

"Oh, this must be some more bad luck," complained Hilda. As she stared down at the skunk, her frown morphed into a smile. "On the other hand, maybe it's *good* luck, because he could be a live subject for our experiments."

Aunt Zelda gaped at her audacious sister. "You want to send a skunk into the Other Realm?"

"Well, it would get their attention." Hilda headed for the stairs. "I won't even have to catch it—I'll leave a trail of bread crumbs into the closet."

"And if you make a false move," said Zelda, "people are going to think that our new perfume is Eau de Skunk."

"Keep the door open . . . I've got some gourmet pretzels he might like." Hilda snuck down the stairs on her tiptoes.

Food! Food! wished Salem, getting delirious when he couldn't find a way to get into the house. Why did they have everything boarded up? He wanted to enter through the back door, which was the quickest way into the kitchen and to the *food!*

Salem didn't want to start mewling or shouting, as that would destroy the illusion of his disguise. That yahoo mob could still be lurking nearby, looking for black cats. Luckily, he wasn't one of *those* anymore.

Hmmm! Maybe Sabrina's window is open. Salem started for the tree near her bedroom window when he suddenly heard a doorknob click. The cat whirled around to see that the back door was now open a crack. *They must have seen me!* He quickly padded into the house, where he was met by a delicious mound of peanuts and crushed pretzels, which he quickly snarfed down.

It's a welcome-home party! he decided. A sumptuous trail of goodies led through the kitchen, and Salem's saliva glands and tastebuds took control of his brain.

"Mmmm. Yum, slurp." He gobbled his way through the kitchen, the living room, and up the stairs, not paying any attention to where he was going. When the pretzels turned into caramel corn, he completely lost his mind.

The last thing Salem remembered was entering a doorway and . . . *zing!* he was transported somewhere else.

"Okay, the skunk is gone," said Aunt Zelda, standing outside the linen closet. "Now what does that prove?"

Aunt Hilda rolled her eyes, looking for an answer. "It proves that living things go somewhere and . . . and pillows do not."

"Do *you* want to take a chance on it?" asked Zelda.

"Both of us can't go," answered Hilda. "Somebody's got to be here for the girls. And when I get around Drell, I tend to forget why I went there. It's probably best that you go. But not now! Give the skunk time to get away."

"Well, I'm glad we got rid of the skunk," said Zelda with a grimace. "I can still *smell* him." She looked hesitantly at the closet door. She was ready to charge off somewhere, but where?

A moment later, Zelda made up her mind. "We can't take the risk of winding up as cosmic dust, so I think we should go to the school and check up on the girls. Who knows what they're dealing with."

"You don't think Salem will ever come home?" asked Hilda forlornly.

Zelda shook her head. "How could he get past all those mortals? No, he'd be crazy to come back to the house. I hope he's far, far away by now."

"Mrrffumble! Mmmumufrrr!" Salem tried to talk, but he was tied up in a net bag. The cat twisted and squirmed, trying to look around, but all he saw were trees and blue sky.

Salem began to sob pitifully. *I was so close to safety! I was in my own little house, eating my own good food. What happened? Where were Hilda and Zelda? Why didn't they save me?*

In desperation, he twisted around like a pretzel and managed to glimpse some strange, metal

structures. He figured he was outdoors somewhere . . . maybe a playground. When he stopped
struggling and listened more closely, he heard the
distant sounds of music, machines whirring, and
children laughing. He finally decided he was at
an amusement park, hidden behind a row of
trailer trucks.

Salem heard a voice that was closer, and he
listened carefully. "Thank you kindly," said the
friendly voice. "Yes, we'll take care of that black
cat for you. Take this slip, and visit our cashier
for your gift certificate. Pleasure doing business
with you."

There was more mumbled conversation from
the other side of the truck, and Salem strained to
catch more. Hanging upside-down in the net, he
saw nothing until the torso of a large man suddenly stepped in front of him. The man had another black cat in a net bag, and the poor kitty
mewled pathetically.

"Get those cats moving!" ordered a voice.
"The big boss will be here any minute. Be careful there! Don't let the cats out of the bags. If
they can't walk, they can't cross your path."

Roughly, a hand grabbed Salem's bag and
lifted him up. The startled kitty tried to claw
back, but it was all so sudden. In seconds, he
found himself stuck inside a truck. At least he
thought he was inside a truck—it was dark,
cold, and musty. More disturbing, there were

dozens of black cats in net bags all around him.

"Eww, that's a smelly one!" complained a voice. "And he's got a white stripe on him. Are you sure that's not a skunk?"

"I found him in that bag," answered the first man. "The white stuff is just paint. Keep him with the others."

Somebody is collecting black cats! thought Salem with alarm.

His imagination ran wild, but he tried to calm himself with logic. These men were going to an awful lot of trouble to collect black cats if they were just planning to get rid of them. It sounded as if they were offering a reward for people who turned in their black cats. *What a heinous thing to do—turning people against their own cats!*

I've got to get out of here! thought Salem. He wasn't scared just for himself anymore—in this superstitious realm, all black cats were threatened with extinction. All good luck was countered by bad luck. Mortals had magic, but they were scared to death of it!

Panting from her long run, Sabrina finally reached the principal's office. When she saw the doorknob looming high overhead, she groaned. *What a dork!* This trip would have taken her thirty seconds at her normal size, but at her teeny size, it had taken her half an hour.

And now she had no way to open the door!

Suddenly, another door farther down the hall-way began to open, and Sabrina pressed against the wall. Everything was so big, it was hard to tell which door it was, but she thought it was the one for the general office. That was where visitors went to check in, and where parents picked up their kids.

One of the cowboys stuck his head out and turned his squinty eyes toward her. Sabrina gasped and held perfectly still, worried that the slightest movement would attract his attention. But he seemed to be looking past her, as if he were waiting for someone to come down the hall.

Then he looked the other way, turning his back to her. Sabrina knew she would have to act fast or miss her chance, so she dashed toward the open door.

Seeing the corridor was empty, the cowboy started to retreat into the office, shutting the door behind him. Sabrina saw the gap growing smaller and smaller, and she put on the afterburners. The space between the door and the doorjamb was almost gone when the teen leaped off her feet and flew through the opening. She tumbled into the carpet just as the door slammed shut behind her, barely missing her legs.

Sabrina sunk down into the plush carpet, which was as tall as a field of wheat. From here, she could see that bounty hunters had overrun the office. They stood on both sides of the counter and were looking over the shoulders of a harried secretary, Mrs. Whitlow, as she studied her computer screen.

"Are you sure you're Dreama's father?" asked Mrs. Whitlow suspiciously. She cast a wary glance at the grizzled cowboy with the black moustache.

"Have you ever seen Dreama's parents?" he asked.

"No," admitted the secretary.

"Then how do you know I'm not her old man?" He gave her a gap-toothed smile. "I really need her for that dentist appointment. Just tell me what class she's in."

The woman quickly turned off the computer screen. "I'll call her on the intercom and tell her to come to the office. If she says you're her dad, then she can go with you."

"Fine. Thank you, ma'am." The cowboy tipped his hat and gave her another toothy smile.

Mrs. Whitlow went into a soundproof booth, and Sabrina could hear her speaking into a microphone. *Wherever you are, Dreama, stay put!* she wanted to shout. But at her present size, all they would hear was a little squeak.

Where is Mr. Kraft when you need him?

One of the cowboys unfurled his lasso and stepped out the door into the corridor. He was probably going to hide and catch Dreama from behind, she figured. The bounty hunters were clever—if they lassoed Dreama and roped her arms to her sides, she couldn't tug on her earlobe and cast a spell. These guys were used to catching witches.

Sabrina realized how lucky she had been to pop her spell in biology class before they got her. She knew she had to warn Dreama, but how?

The tiny witch lifted her head above the carpet and peered around the room. Mrs. Whitlow walked out of the broadcast booth, and Sabrina wondered if she had left the microphone on. She took off running through the high carpet, trying not to trip over the occasional paper clip or staple.

Running at full speed, Sabrina charged through the door and into the booth, just as Mrs. Whitlow shut the door. Once again the door clipped Sabrina's heels and sent her sprawling into a morass of carpet. "I've got to quit doing that," she muttered to herself.

But now she was alone with the intercom, which rested on a desk a hundred feet over her head, or so it looked. *I can't stay this size any longer,* thought Sabrina, *but I'll have to be very careful about how I word the reverse spell.*

After a moment, she pointed her finger at herself and said, "I'd rather be tall, I'd rather be small. But regular I don't want to be at all!"

Sabrina held her breath as she felt her body

changing. When she opened her eyes, she was very relieved to find that she was back to her regular size, and still alone inside the soundproof booth.

She plunked down in the chair and looked at the old-fashioned soundboard. Why was Mr. Kraft too cheap to buy anything new? With a shrug, she pushed all the trimpot slides forward, then she pressed the big button on the microphone.

Loud speakers in the hallways, classrooms, lunchroom, and teachers' lounge squealed with a horrible shriek of feedback. Everyone in the whole school howled and covered their ears. Before the squeal even died down, Sabrina's voice was booming all over the building:

"Dreama! Look out for the cowboys. Meet me at my locker. *Hurry!*"

She clicked off the switch just as the door opened, and a steely-eyed cowboy regarded her. "Well, Missy, it's time for you to come with us."

When he tossed his lasso at her, Sabrina whirled around in her chair and ducked. The lasso settled over the back of her chair, and the cowboy yanked hard, pulling the chair right into his stomach. As he doubled over, Sabrina slipped past him into the office.

Lassoes flew through the air, but they collided over her head, turning into a knotted mess. Her luck held out as she ducked through the door into the hallway. Laying rubber with her tennis shoes, Sabrina took a sharp right and headed for her locker. She could hear shouts and pounding cowboy boots right behind her.

Sabrina turned a corner, and a familiar voice cut through the din. "Miss Spellman! Were you playing with my intercom?"

Mr. Kraft! Sabrina kept running, but she glanced over her shoulder to see the cowboys careen around the corner, lassoes twirling, only to crash into Mr. Kraft. All of them ended up on the floor in a heap of arms, legs, and ropes. Sabrina patted the horseshoe nail in her pocket for more good luck, then hurried on.

Rounding another corner, she saw Dreama leaning against her locker. Waving frantically, Sabrina ran up to her. "We've got to get out of here!"

Dreama yawned. "Did you call me? Everything was so confusing that I took a little nap in the girls' locker room."

Sabrina heard shouts behind her, and she turned to see the posse of cowboys come skidding around the corner. Immediately she grabbed Dreama's hand and ran for the back door. "Gotta go!"

The cowboys chased after them, but all Sabrina could hear was Mr. Kraft yelling, "I warn you cowboys—you're all getting detention!"

It was a mad rush for the back door, but Dreama and Sabrina were in the lead. The girls charged out the back door of the school and found themselves inside a corral, surrounded by horses and mules.

"Oh, right," said Dreama. "The horseshoe laboratory."

"Grab a horse," said Sabrina, reaching out for one of the large four-legged beasts.

"But I don't know how to ride!" protested Dreama.

"Start learning."

The door suddenly opened, and two of the cowboys stumbled out. Dreama still didn't move with much urgency.

"Remember," said Sabrina, "they want to capture you and turn you into a toad."

"Oh, right!" exclaimed Dreama. With an impressive leap, the lanky witch landed on the back of a horse and gripped his mane. "Giddyup!" she cried.

Astride her mount, Dreama charged toward the fence and leaped over it with a single bound. She kept right on galloping across the schoolyard. Sabrina blinked in amazement, and so did the cowboys.

More cowboys spilled out of the door, including the black-moustachioed leader. Then Mr. Kraft stumbled out, but Sabrina saw he was tightly bound with lassoes.

"Get her!" shouted Black Moustache, pointing at Sabrina.

Sabrina tried to make like Dreama and leap on top of a horse; but the horse moved at the last moment, and she landed in the mud. Suddenly lassoes flashed through the air, falling around her shoulders. A split-second later, Sabrina was trussed up like a Thanksgiving turkey.

"Help!" she screamed.

"No, Harv," shouted Diane Abernathy, pull, pull, Sabrina.

She managed to make her Diane and put on top of a horse, but the horse moved at the last moment and she landed in the mud. Suddenly very much in the way of the false rumor. A few seconds later, Sabrina was moved to the a... carrying rider from the screen.

Chapter 8

☆

☆

The bounty hunter with the black moustache strolled up to Sabrina, gazed down at her on the ground, and gave her a nasty grin. She struggled against the ropes that bound her arms to her sides, but it was no use. She wasn't going anywhere.

"You led us a merry chase, Missy, but your luck has run out." He motioned to his confederates. "Let's ride back to the house and catch the other one. Pinto, you get this one back to the boss."

"Yes, sir," growled a stocky cowboy with an eyepatch. He looked a bit like a pirate Sabrina knew.

"Just a moment!" called an indignant voice. Mr. Kraft staggered toward them, his arms also bound to his sides. "How dare you chase my students and lasso them!" Then he thought for a moment. "Can you teach me how to do that?"

"We're busy," grumbled the leader of the bounty hunters. He strode away from the principal and grabbed a horse.

"But we've been looking for people like you!" shouted Mr. Kraft, chasing after them. "How would you like to be substitute teachers?"

One of the cowboys stuck out a spur and tripped Mr. Kraft, who tumbled helplessly to the ground. With lassoes wrapped all around him, he couldn't move—he just lay there like a beached walrus. The cowboys laughed at him while they gathered up some horses. Pinto grabbed Sabrina by the scruff of her neck and dragged her roughly to her feet.

Suddenly a voice thundered across the schoolyard. "Unhand that girl! And pick up that principal, too."

Sabrina looked up and saw Aunt Hilda and Aunt Zelda striding toward them across the schoolyard. They stopped a safe distance away from the bounty hunters, but a fire burned in their eyes. Reverse spells or not, they were going to start throwing magic around.

"Darling!" shouted Mr. Kraft.

Aunt Zelda scowled. "Don't worry, Sweetie, we'll get you out of there. Sabrina, step away from that chubby one, because he's going to get it first."

Sabrina dashed away from Pinto, who made a lunge for her but was too slow. He backed off and let her escape, unwilling to get too close to the angry witches.

Black Moustache waved his hand warily at them. "Hey, you two aren't on the list anymore. Let us have the young ones, and we'll go happily."

Hilda frowned unhappily. "Black Bart, I'm surprised you're doing this . . . after all we meant to each other."

The leader of the bounty hunters looked chastened as he kicked the ground with his boot. "Aw, Hilda, you're not going to make it personal, are you? It's just a job—"

"I'll give them a job!" shouted Mr. Kraft from the ground. "How about hall monitors? Flexible hours!"

Zelda stepped closer to her beloved, Mr. Kraft. "Let all of them go and take *us* instead. We'll stand in for them at the Witches' Council. It's perfectly legal. Besides, Dreama isn't even a full-fledged witch yet."

"Yeah!" insisted Hilda. "Let's talk to Drell and see what we can do to stop this madness. Turning Dreama into a toad, even if you can do it, is not going to solve anything."

Black Bart brushed his moustache back.

"Well, I suppose that is legal. We'll get our bounty either way."

"Don't do it," Sabrina begged her aunts. "There's got to be another way."

"Ssshh!" hissed Hilda out of the side of her mouth. "We want to see how they get back to the Other Realm. You take off and find Dreama. And reverse the spell, will ya?"

"Okay, thanks." Sabrina gave each of her aunts an urgent hug and rushed off. "Reverse the spell! Reverse the spell!" she chanted to herself. It was a tough job, but somebody had to do it.

Daylight suddenly streamed into the back of the truck, blinding Salem for a moment. He squinted into the light and saw the silhouette of a large man darkening the doorway. A voice behind him said, "There they are, boss. Shall we take them to the others?"

"Ew!" said a deep voice that Salem definitely recognized. "What stinks so badly in there?"

"One of them may be a skunk," said another man.

The boss shook his fist and thundered, "You can't tell the difference between a skunk and a cat? What kind of morons have I got working for me? Don't answer that."

"I found him bagged up and ready to go," said another helper. "I think he got into some white paint and got sprayed by a skunk."

"Hmmm," said their leader thoughtfully. "If he's a cat, maybe he's a *smart* cat. All cats aren't what they seem, you know. Drag him out here."

"Okay, boss!"

Salem tried not to get too excited, because he was about to see a face he hated. He was probably in worse trouble now than when the mob was chasing him.

"Hold him up," ordered the boss. "Careful there. Don't damage him."

A moment later, Salem came eye to eye with Drell, master warlock, president of the Witches' Council. He was the one who had personally turned Salem into a cat for his punishment, after stripping away his magic.

"Do I detect a familiar face?" asked Drell with a grin. "Nice disguise, Salem."

"Mrrffumble! Mmmumufrrr!" responded the cat. Drell gripped him by the neck and opened the bag, accidentally yanking his whiskers. "Yeow!" howled Salem. "If I want a shave, I'll go to a barber, thank you!"

The helpers leaped back, gasping with surprise. Drell ignored them to concentrate on the cat. "Salem, old friend, this is a pleasant surprise. How could you have let these bumblers capture you?"

"I didn't," protested Salem. "I went into the linen closet in our house and ended up *here*."

Drell chuckled. "Ah, yes. Through much trial

and error, we finally figured out the reverse spell works on the portals. They take you to the place you would least like to be. And if you don't know what that is, the magic chooses for you. So here you are, Salem—my captive. I wouldn't have cared before, but now you're valuable."

"Why am I valuable?" muttered Salem. "I bring nothing but bad luck, even to myself."

Drell pointed outside the door at the amusement park. "Thanks to those meddling teenage witches, it's a new world out there. You aren't born with magic powers anymore, you have to *collect* them, like you collect baseball cards. So far, everyone is looking for good luck, but they don't realize the potential in bad luck. It's a growth industry! With this black cat racket, I'm going to corner the market on bad luck."

"That's diabolically fiendish," said Salem. "If people don't give their good-luck charms to you, you turn the black cats loose on them. Congratulations, Drell, what a scam! Do you want a feline partner?"

"I was thinking that I would need a liaison between me and all these cats," answered Drell, motioning around at the squirming bags filling the trailer truck. "You're just the man . . . er, cat for the job."

"Well, cut me down from here, and let's draw up our marketing plan," said Salem, squirming eagerly.

"Not so fast," replied Drell. "My beeper is going off, which means some more of your family members have turned up. There's a slim chance we can get things back to normal, and you'll be worthless again. But having you in custody will help me deal with your family."

"You cad!" exclaimed Salem with a certain amount of admiration.

"I've got to maintain my position in the brave new world," explained Drell. He waved to his minions. "Okay, boys, take this load to the pit. Give them food and water—we've got to keep them healthy. You can give a little extra to Salem, but don't let him cross your path."

Drell shoved Salem back into his bag and tossed him to a man on the truck. A moment later, Salem was surrounded by darkness and frightened cats, as the truck rumbled through the city. They were on their way to the pit, which sounded like more bad luck.

Sabrina pulled the blinds shut on the windows in her bedroom and began to pace. Even though nobody was after them at the moment, she was still nervous. "Aunt Hilda and Aunt Zelda have bought us some time," said Sabrina, "but we've got to find a way to reverse the spell."

Dreama sat on the bed and folded her hands, thinking intently. "I know this is my fault, and I want to do something to help. But the football team has to share the blame, too! If it wasn't for their smelly superstitions, I wouldn't have tried to teach them a lesson. Now they're so conceited, they don't even practice anymore! Everyone is so certain they'll win."

"And they smell worse than ever," muttered Sabrina. Her shoulders slumped, and her face turned gloomy. Then she thought about what Dreama had just said. "It all began with the football players, didn't it?"

"Yes, without them, no wonderland of superstitions."

"Then it's got to *end* with them, too," declared Sabrina. "If they lose a game in front of all those fans, then everyone will know their superstitions are worthless. Aunt Zelda even said it before everything went crazy—the only way to stop the superstition is for them to *lose* a football game."

Dreama jumped up the from the bed. "They play again in two nights! But do you really think it will work on the whole Mortal Realm?"

"We've got to start somewhere. If any part of a spell fails, then the whole spell is broken. I remember that from the quiz for my witch's license."

"And if one person stops believing, maybe all of them will," concluded Dreama. Then she shook her head. "To pull this off, we're going to need a lot of luck."

Sabrina grinned. "I've got that covered. I overheard Mr. Kraft tell a teacher that he had a whole bunch of horseshoes locked up in his office. Maybe we could, uh . . . borrow a few."

"Let's borrow them all," said Dreama. "If it weren't for me, they wouldn't be worth anything."

Aunt Zelda looked around at the dismal warehouse, wondering what they were doing here. Except for a few old crates, the vast storage room was empty. A row of windows under the roof were all broken. It looked as if nobody had been here in years, except for the grubby cowboys who had brought them here.

The bounty hunters had built a campfire in one corner of the cavernous building, and they were lying around on their sleeping bags, eating baked beans out of cans. This left Zelda and Hilda with nothing to do but pace the dusty floor, and worry. They sure didn't want to get too close to the cowboys.

After a few minutes, Black Bart came through the door at the end of the building. Zelda waved accusingly at him. "What did you do with Mr. Kraft?"

"I took him home and put him to bed," answered the bounty hunter. "He'd had a long day, and I convinced him that everything that happened was caused by bad luck. He's going to take a couple of days off. To make him feel better, I told him that my boys would work in the lunchroom."

"What are we doing here, anyway?" asked Aunt Hilda impatiently. "This is a strange place to wait for Drell. We're not even in the Other Realm!"

"Who said you were going to the Other Realm? This is the place where all the action is." Black Bart turned toward the door. "Wait a minute, I think I hear the boss's car."

Hilda whispered to her sister, "Something weird is going on here. Drell never rides around in a car, and he hates the Mortal Realm."

"This is not the same Mortal Realm we're used to," Zelda reminded her.

A big man in a fancy, sequined cowboy suit strolled through the door. Upon seeing Hilda and Zelda, his arms opened wide in warm recognition. "Ah, my two favorite witches! How nice to see you here!"

"I wish I could say the same thing," answered Zelda. She looked at Hilda, who was flirting and smiling at Drell. "Stick to business."

Drell immediately took Hilda's hand and bent down to kiss it. "Enchanted, as always, my dear. I wish we had time to party, but I'm afraid your boring sister is right—we must stick to business."

Hilda nearly swooned, then her demeanor turned deadly serious. "Okay, here's the deal:

You leave Sabrina and Dreama alone to try to reverse the spell, and we'll go before the Witches' Council instead of them."

Drell smiled with amusement. "Nice try. Here's the reality. It's hard for witches to get around these days, so I'm the council until further notice. In fact, witches' magic is very unpredictable, while this new mortal magic is quite effective, if you know how to use it."

"Then you're not holding a grudge," said Hilda brightly.

"Personally, no." The warlock scowled and pointed his finger at them. "But somebody has to pay for this mess, because every witch I know is ticked off. My advisers tell me the punishment spell should work despite everything else, so Dreama has two more days to turn herself in. If she doesn't show, the two of you will become toads in her place."

He smiled sympathetically. "Tell you what, we'll halve the sentence, and you'll only be toads for five hundred years each."

"Oh, thanks," grumbled Hilda, crossing her arms.

"What if the girls manage to reverse the spell?" asked Zelda.

Drell laughed out loud. "Right! I have the greatest minds in the Other Realm working on it, and they're stumped. There's no way, but if Dreama can reverse the spell, we'll let her off with a stern lecture. Otherwise, you'll serve her punishment for her. Listen, ladies, I think you'll have great lives here in the Mortal Realm as toads, because toads are mostly considered good luck. Of course, you will give warts to everybody who touches you."

"I'm going to give you warts where you've never seen warts!" promised Hilda.

Drell chuckled and started for the door, then he stopped and looked back. "May I remind you, you're here under the witches' honor system, so don't even think about escaping. You should also know that I've got your familiar. Salem is working for *me* now."

"Bad Luck Incorporated?" asked Zelda.

"Something like that. I'll leave a couple of bounty hunters just to keep you company." Drell waved to the cowboys, and most of them followed him out. Bart and another one stayed behind, and they closed and locked the door after the departing warlock.

"It didn't take him much time to move in," said Zelda with disgust.

"He's attracted to magic," answered Hilda, "and this is where the magic is. It's making everybody a little crazy."

"I like Dreama, but I don't really want to become a toad for her." Aunt Zelda frowned and kicked at some dust on the warehouse floor. "Even if they are good luck."

"I know," said Aunt Hilda, wringing her hands. "And I don't look good in warts. I can't help feeling that all of this is because of that shoelace I broke."

As soon as the sun went down, and a late autumn chill fell over the town of Westbridge, Sabrina and Dreama tiptoed to the high school. They circled around to the rear of the building, where there was a row of large frosted windows. All the lights were out, and even the horses and mules seemed to be asleep.

Neither one of them liked sneaking into the school after dark, but they couldn't trust their witchcraft. They needed mucho luck in order to cast a spell that would cause the football team to lose. Sabrina gripped her flashlight and followed Dreama up to the outer wall.

"Are you sure you left the window unlocked," Sabrina asked nervously.

"For the tenth time," said Dreama, "I left it unlocked. When I went in there to take a nap, it was kind of musty, so I opened the window a crack."

Dreama found the slightly open window without any problem, and she motioned to Sabrina. But the teenage witch froze in her tracks, a stricken look on her face.

"What's the matter now?" asked Dreama impatiently. "We're only going to borrow them for a little while. Besides, if we're successful, old horseshoes will be worthless again."

"It's not the horseshoes I feel guilty about," answered Sabrina glumly. "It's making Harvey's team lose. They've waited so long to have a decent team."

"They'll still have the same team they had before," answered Dreama. "Only now they'll know it was *them* winning the games, not their dirty T-shirts. We're doing them a favor."

"Why don't I think they would look at it that way?" Sabrina shook off her feelings of guilt, grabbed the window, and opened it all the way. "Okay, you go first."

Dreama had an easier time crawling through the opening, but she fell off and tumbled onto the floor with a thud.

"I'm okay," she whispered to Sabrina. Dreama moved a bench under the window, so that her partner would have an easier time getting over.

Dreama is a little flighty, but she means well, Sabrina told herself. She tried to remember all the dumb spells she had cast when she was still learning. Some recent ones weren't so smart either. Being a witch was a heavy responsibility, with a lot of important rules, and Dreama had to learn not to cast spells carelessly.

Once they were inside the school, they had no trouble finding Mr. Kraft's office, but the door was locked. "Stand back," whispered Sabrina, rolling up her sleeves. "I'm going to use magic to open it."

She felt relatively safe using a spell that was easy to reverse. When she cast a spell to lock the door, it promptly unlocked; and they walked right in.

"Oh, my gosh!" exclaimed Dreama. Mr. Kraft's entire desk was covered in a mound of horseshoes of all shapes and sizes. Some were new, and some were old and bent with nails still in them. His office looked like a miniature blacksmith shop, with tools, nails, a bellows, and even a small anvil.

On top of the pile of horseshoes was a note, and Sabrina snatched it and read it. "Listen to this," she told Dreama. "It's a memo from Mrs. Whitlow in the office. Mr. Kraft called and will be taking two days of vacation. His office is to be left undisturbed—no one can go in."

"But we're already in."

"And we're going to stay in," concluded Sabrina. "We'll stay right here until the football game." She ran her hands through the clattering mound of old horseshoes. "This good luck is not leaving our sight—we're going to need it to beat the smelly socks."

Chapter 9

☆

It was the night of another big football game, but Harvey Kinkle wasn't nervous at all. He was never nervous before a football game anymore, or hardly even excited. He wouldn't tell his coach or teammates, but football wasn't quite as fun when you knew you were going to win.

More than once, he had thought about taking a shower and changing his socks, but he couldn't let the team down, or his best friend, Brad. *Isn't this what every football team wants? Victory after victory. We don't even have to play well, just run the plays.*

Brad slapped him on the back, knocking him out of his gloomy reverie. Harvey looked up and realized that he was in the hallway at school, and the last bell of the day had just rung. Everyone would be heading to the football field soon, to watch another great victory they didn't deserve.

"What's the matter with you?" asked Brad. "It's game day—put on your game face."

"Sure," said Harvey, mustering a bland smile.

All of a sudden, they heard laughter coming from the other end of the hallway. Harvey and Brad turned to see students pointing at something, then stepping aside to let them pass. A clanging sound echoed in the hallway.

As the procession drew closer, Harvey couldn't believe his eyes—it was Sabrina and Dreama, and they were covered in horseshoes. They looked and sounded like knights in armor as they clanked down the hall. They walked like knights too, stiff-legged and stiff-armed. The horseshoes seemed to be crocheted together with bits of wire, like old chain mail.

"Hi, Sabrina!" yelled Brad cheerfully. He grabbed Harvey and pushed him down the hall. "Hey, that is a really cool good-luck costume! The team doesn't need it, but it's the thought that counts."

"We wanted to show our support!" said Sabrina with a big smile. She glanced at Harvey, but she seemed to be avoiding his eyes. "You can't have too much good luck, can you?"

"No way," agreed Brad. "Hey, see you at the

game. Afterwards, we'll sit outside the Slicery and eat some victory pizza, as usual."

"Sounds good," said Sabrina, clanking off down the hall with Dreama following.

Brad shook his head in amazement. "Who else would wear a suit of horseshoes for her guy? Do you know how heavy that must be?" He slapped Harvey on the back. "Man, you have the coolest girlfriend."

"Yeah, I do," agreed Harvey. He glanced back at Sabrina with a bittersweet smile. "I don't get to see her much anymore."

"That's because she's one of *them*," whispered Brad.

Harvey looked quizzically at him, and Brad added, "You know, she still takes a bath."

"Oh, yeah." Harvey sniffed under his armpits and tried not to gag. "Not like us."

"We're beyond that now," said Brad proudly. "Stop looking so bummed out—there's no way we can lose. What could possibly go wrong?"

Harvey tried to laugh, although he was more sad than happy. "Yeah, what could possibly go wrong?"

"Okay, cats, I'm leading a revolt out of here!" declared Salem to the hundreds of black cats stuck down in the pit with him. That didn't stop their mewling and bawling for one second, but Salem felt better for saying it.

Salem looked around at the teeming mass of cats. He knew he could stay here and do Drell's bidding—and have a semi-comfortable life—but he couldn't stand to be around this many miserable cats. Cats weren't designed to be held captive—they needed to be *free*.

"There's strength in numbers!" he told the cats, who continued to ignore him. "I will be your Spartacus and lead you in the revolt. We'll spread bad luck throughout the realm!"

It sounded like a good idea to him. Of course, first they had to get out of here. As far as he could tell, they were in a slag pit inside an old foundry. There was a hard mound of industrial waste in one corner, but it wasn't high enough to climb out. Several of the cats had tried to jump out by standing on the heap, but they had fallen just short.

"We need a feline chain," he told the cats. He started the process by jumping on top of the slag heap and stretching as far as he could against the wall. Cats like to stretch, so soon he was surrounded by about a dozen cats stretching along with him. Salem picked the biggest cat and jumped on his shoulders.

"Hold still!" he ordered the cat when he tried to move. "The rest of you! Come on!" It took a while, but the cats eventually figured out what he wanted. By climbing on one anothers' shoulders, they formed a pyramid that reached all the way to the top. They looked like a bunch of kitty cheerleaders, but it worked. Other cats crawled over their shoulders and escaped over the top.

"Don't forget about the rest of us!" ordered Salem, who was still near the bottom. He needn't have worried, because the clever cats pushed a long board into the pit, and they soon had a ramp to climb out. Five minutes later, the pit was empty, and two hundred black cats were milling around the old foundry.

Drell was stupid, Salem decided, because he hadn't left a guard. Salem found an old window with a broken pane of glass, and he led the cats outside. It was night, and the factory complex was dark and deserted. Nobody noticed a couple hundred black cats dash across the parking lot and escape into the street.

Salem could see bright lights glimmering in the distance. He didn't know it was the high school football stadium, filled with fans, but it looked like civilization.

"Follow me!" he shouted, leading the herd of black cats toward the glittering lights.

Sabrina and Dreama clinked to a stop at the top of the bleachers in the visitor's end zone. It was the only part of the stadium that wasn't filled to capacity with fans eager to see their lucky Scallions win again. The mascot was wearing his vegetable suit, and he was covered in four-leaf clovers. Half the crowd carried wooden salad bowls to knock on during the crucial moments.

Therefore, Sabrina and Dreama fit right in with their horseshoe armor, although sitting down proved to be difficult. Taking the last and highest row in the bleachers, they found they could lean against the railing without tipping over. They also had a distant but good view of the game.

"Listen, Dreama," said Sabrina, "this is going to require that you actually understand football. There's a scoreboard way down there . . . see it?"

Dreama frowned. "Oh, no, I was afraid it was going to come to this."

The game was half over by the time Sabrina had explained football well enough to Dreama that she could understand who was winning. As usual, it was the Fighting Scallions, leading by one touchdown in a lackluster game. The Sunnyside Cougars had just punted for the umpteenth time, and the Scallions had it on their own twenty yard line. The crowd cheered lustily as the grubby home team went on offense.

"Okay, let's give it a try," whispered Sabrina. "All we have to do is cast a spell that the Scallions will win, even though we want them to lose. It's all reversed, right?"

"It sure is," agreed Dreama. She tugged on her earlobe and said, "In thick or thin, Scallions will win."

"And if they lose, we'll get the blues," finished Sabrina. With her finger, she directed a jolt of magic toward the field, where a play was unfolding.

"And it's a hand-off to Brad Alcerro!" said the stadium announcer, "He's going to his right. Oooh, he's hit hard at the line, and the ball pops loose! It's a *fumble*."

Clanking loudly, Sabrina sat forward to see one of the red-shirted Cougars scoop up the ball and run an easy twenty yards into the end zone. "It's a Cougar touchdown, and the game is tied," stated a surprised announcer to a stunned crowd.

Sabrina looked at Dreama and winked. "We're in business."

All of a sudden, the football game turned interesting; the Cougars played as if they had a chance to win, and the Scallions played as if they had a chance to lose. The complacent crowd cheered lustily when something good happened, and they stroked their rabbits' feet when bad luck befell their heroes. The girls didn't use their magic again, hoping the first spell had been enough.

Too quickly they were down to the closing seconds of the game. The Fighting Scallions were down by four points, but they were driving with the ball. In fact, they seemed to have rallied both their good luck and their football skills.

As the clock ticked down the closing minute,

the Scallions quarterback handed the ball to Brad. He scampered twenty-three yards for a first-down in Cougar territory, and the Scallions called a time-out.

"Where was the weak-side lineback on that play?" ranted Dreama. "That number fifty-four should be on the chess team!"

"Calm down," said Sabrina nervously, "we've still got a chance to cast a spell. Remember, make it for the Scallions to win."

"Good man-to-man in the secondary would help, too," said Dreama with disgust. "But okay, I'm ready."

"Eight seconds left in the game," said the announcer. "Just time for one more play. The Scallions will have to go for the end zone."

The fans were knocking on the wooden bowls, stroking their rabbits' feet, and kissing their four-leaf clovers. But they looked stunned as they went through these motions, as if they had begun to doubt superstitions.

"Same as before," said Dreama. She yanked on her earlobe and said, "In thick or thin, Scallions will win."

"And if they lose, we'll get the blues," added Sabrina, shooting a spark with her finger.

"Hut!" cried the quarterback. He scrambled back and lifted his arm to throw a pass. The final seconds were ticking off the game clock, and the play seemed to unfold in slow motion. Sabrina saw Harvey running down the sideline, wide open, and Dreama was muttering about blown coverage.

The quarterback finally spotted Harvey, and he hurled the ball just as Cougar defenders pummeled him. It was a good pass—straight and true—and Harvey sprinted to meet the ball. Unless he dropped it, thought Sabrina, a touchdown was certain.

Out of the dark sky came a bolt of lightning, which struck the football in mid-air, exploding it like a bucket of confetti. Harvey reached to catch the ball, but all he got was a handful of smoke and smoldering bits of leather. He tumbled to the ground, grasping at the nebulous embers.

The crowd gasped in unison, just as the timer's gun shot off, ending the game. Westbridge coaches argued with the officials, but the referees rushed to escape from the field. The Cougar players jumped up and down, slapping each other on the back over their miraculous victory. Sabrina wondered if they would ever take a bath again.

Nothing looked different about the autumn night and the glowing football stadium, except that the crowd was silent. Some of them threw away their rabbits' feet, and Mrs. Quick crunched her lucky wishbone. The Westbridge loss had been shocking, but somehow it didn't seem enough to stop the belief in superstitions.

Then a murmur rose up from the crowd, and it slowly turned into shrieks and screams of terror. People in the stands jumped up and tried to run, but there was no place to escape from the horror that was sweeping over the stadium.

Dreama grabbed Sabrina by the shoulder and shook her, rattling all her horseshoes. "Look! Look!" she shouted. "Down on the field."

Sabrina finally twisted around enough in her armor to see where Dreama was pointing. Incredibly, hundreds of black cats were storming the field, chasing huge football players and the throngs of people who had run onto the field. Like an oil slick, the black cats slid across the green field, then the harbingers of doom scattered throughout the bleachers. They crossed everyone's path—there was no escape from the onslaught of bad luck.

Like everyone else in the large crowd, Sabrina held her breath, waiting to see what would happen next. Surely, the stands would collapse, or there'd be a tornado. Instead, everyone just looked at one another, unable to believe that nothing was happening.

"It worked!" squealed Dreama. Then she cast off her incredible suit of horseshoes, which seemed to be the signal that the reign of superstition was officially over. Everyone threw down their good-luck charms, acting as if they'd been freed from slavery. Even the football players stripped off their dirty jerseys and ran for the showers.

"Sabrina! Sabrina!" called a familiar voice. It was Salem! People actually patted the cat on the back as he bounded up the stairs toward Sabrina. With a purr of happiness, Salem leaped into her arms and tried to snuggle, without much luck.

He looked scornfully at the suit of horseshoes she was wearing. "Pretty bad, was it?"

"Yes, but it's good now!" She squeezed her kitty with such force that the horseshoe nails started sticking him.

"Help! Ouch! Eeek!" yelled the cat. "Easy with the Iron Maiden costume."

"We need to find Hilda, Zelda, and Drell," said Sabrina. "Right now."

A moment later, the two witches and the cat disappeared, leaving behind a pile of horseshoes that clattered loudly onto the metal bleachers.

They reappeared inside on old, grungy warehouse, which had no furniture except for a card table. Seated around the card table were her Aunt Zelda, Aunt Hilda, and two of the bounty hunters. As Sabrina stepped closer, she could see that one of the cowboys was Black Bart, leader of the posse, and they were playing cards.

"I bid three no trump," said Black Bart.

His partner, Aunt Hilda, frowned at him. "Can

you really make three no trump? Because if you can't, I—"

"Aunt Hilda! Aunt Zelda!" called Sabrina, rushing toward her beloved aunts. There was a wonderful reunion, and nobody got more kisses and hugs than Salem.

"I hate to ask," said Dreama, "but where is Drell?"

Zelda held up a small cage, which enclosed an especially ugly, fat, warty toad. "Do you see this handsome fellow?" she asked. "This is Drell. At the appointed hour, he went to turn *us* into toads. He carefully reversed the spell, but somehow the backfire spell didn't backfire, and it worked on him. Now I know that was caused by *you*, reversing the original spell. So Drell is a toad without any magical powers."

"We thought we'd leave him that way for a while," said Hilda with a satisfied smile. "Or until a beautiful princess kisses him, which is highly unlikely."

"Ribbit!" called the toad plaintively, hopping in Hilda's direction. Zelda quickly put the cage back on the floor.

"I lost my bad-luck mojo," mused Salem, "but at least I still have my pot of gold from the rainbow!"

"No, you don't," said Zelda. "When this realm reverted back to normal, all the stuff caused by magical luck disappeared. To the mortals, it will be like it never happened."

"Uh-oh," murmured Sabrina. "Somebody is feeling awfully low right now, and I need to console him. Gotta go."

"Do you want me to come with you?" asked Dreama.

"No, I can take care of this by myself." Sabrina whirled her finger in the air, disappearing in a column of sparkling lights.

Sabrina stepped out of the bushes at the back door of the high school just as the last of the football players straggled out of the locker room. There were no throngs of cheering fans, and the players looked gloomy and dejected, but they were at least clean. Showers and shavers had been running after the loss, but there would be no victory party.

As soon as she saw Harvey, with a bruise on his face and a limp in his stride, Sabrina rushed to his side and grabbed his arm. "Sweetie, are you all right? You smell super!"

"We lost," he muttered, still in shock. "I never saw anything like that before. I had the ball right in my hands—it was a sure six points. Then a lightning bolt shot out of the sky and destroyed the ball!"

"These things happen," said Sabrina.

"They do?" He shook his head. "I thought our luck would hold out."

"Your luck is holding out." Sabrina reached

into her pocket and pulled out a sprig of green moss, which she held over their heads. "It's close enough to Christmas for mistletoe, isn't it?"

Harvey grinned. "I think so." He took Sabrina in his arms and kissed her, and she let the mistletoe flutter to the ground.

About the Author

JOHN VORNHOLT has had several writing and performing careers, ranging from being a stuntman to writing animated cartoons, but he enjoys writing books most of all. He likes playing one-on-one with the reader. John has written more than a dozen *Star Trek* books, plus novels set in such diverse universes as *Babylon 5* and *Alex Mack*. His fantasy novel about Aesop, *The Fabulist*, is being adapted as a musical for the stage.

John presently lives in Arizona with his wife, Nancy, and two kids, Sarah and Eric, and he goes roller-skating three times a week.

Send e-mail to John at: jbv@azstarnet.com

YOU DON'T WANT TO MISS ANY ISSUES!

☐ **SABRINA**
Six-Issue
Comic Book
Subscription **$7.50**
($8.50-CANADA)

THAT'S A TOTAL SAVINGS OF $3.24!

☐ **SPECIAL OFFER** sso
THE FIRST TWENTY ISSUES of
SABRINA THE TEENAGE WITCH in one
COMPLETE PACKAGE
(THAT'S A $33 VALUE)
FOR ONLY **$21.95**
($25.95-CANADA)

(Shipping & handling included)

TOTAL
AMOUNT
ENCLOSED $ _____

Sabrina Subscription Offer

ARCHIE COMIC PUBLICATIONS, INC. P.O. Box #573, Mamaroneck, NY 10543-0573

NAME _____ AGE ____ MALE ☐ FEMALE ☐
(PLEASE PRINT)

ADDRESS _____

CITY _____ STATE ____ ZIP+4 ____ - ____

DAYTIME PHONE # _____

☐ VISA ☐ MASTERCARD

[ ][ ][ ][ ][ ][ ][ ][ ][ ][ ][ ][ ][ ][ ][ ][ ]   EXP. DATE ___/___
                                                    MO. YR.

SIGNATURE _____

AVAILABLE IN U.S. & CANADA ONLY. All orders must be payable in U.S. funds
PLEASE ALLOW 6-8 WEEKS DELIVERY.

9001   TM & © 1990 Archie Comic Publications, Inc.   ARCMX

Put a little magic in your everyday life!

Magic Handbook

Patricia Barnes-Svarney

Sabrina has a Magic Handbook, full of spells and rules to help her learn to control her magic. Now you can have your own Magic Handbook, full of tricks and everyday experiments you can do to find the magic that's inside and all around you!

From Archway Paperbacks
Published by Pocket Books

2021-02

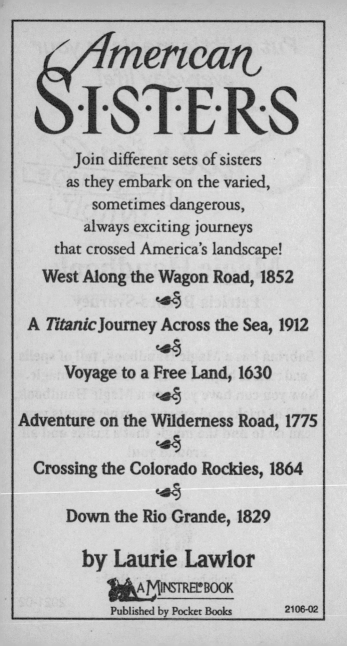

American SISTERS

Join different sets of sisters
as they embark on the varied,
sometimes dangerous,
always exciting journeys
that crossed America's landscape!

West Along the Wagon Road, 1852

❧

A *Titanic* Journey Across the Sea, 1912

❧

Voyage to a Free Land, 1630

❧

Adventure on the Wilderness Road, 1775

❧

Crossing the Colorado Rockies, 1864

❧

Down the Rio Grande, 1829

by Laurie Lawlor

A MINSTREL® BOOK

Published by Pocket Books

2106-02